"Until the police can free up someone to guard you, you're coming with me."

His authoritative tone that just five minutes ago she'd thought was reassuring now raised her hackles. "And I don't have any say-so in this?"

"Nope."

A splinter of fear stabbed her. "Why? What's happened?" Resa knew how much Archer valued his privacy. How desperately he wanted to bury himself in that basement firing range of his and never come out.

There was only one reason he'd give all that up. Only one reason he'd even consider taking on the responsibility of keeping her safe.

He thought he had the chance to catch the man who'd destroyed his life....

MALLORY KANE

SILENT GUARDIAN

HARLEQUIN®

TORONTO • NEW YORK • LONDON
AMSTERDAM • PARIS • SYDNEY • HAMBURG
STOCKHOLM • ATHENS • TOKYO • MILAN • MADRID
PRAGUE • WARSAW • BUDAPEST • AUCKLAND

This book is dedicated to Tina Colombo,
whose help and encouragement have meant
more to me than she can possibly know.

ISBN-13: 978-0-373-69304-7
ISBN-10:   0-373-69304-4

SILENT GUARDIAN

www.eHarlequin.com

Printed in U.S.A.

ABOUT THE AUTHOR

Mallory Kane credits her love of books to her mother, a librarian, who taught her that books are a precious resource and should be treated with loving respect. Her father and grandfather were steeped in the Southern tradition of oral history, and they could hold an audience spellbound for hours with their storytelling skills. Mallory aspires to be as good a storyteller as her father.

She loves romantic suspense with dangerous heroes and dauntless heroines and often uses her medical background to add an extra dose of intrigue to her books. Another fascination that she enjoys exploring in her reading and writing is the infinite capacity of the brain to adapt and develop higher skills.

Mallory lives in Mississippi with her computer-genius husband, their two fascinating cats and, at current count, seven computers.

She loves to hear from readers. You can write her at rickey_m@bellsouth.net or via Harlequin Books.

Books by Mallory Kane

CAST OF CHARACTERS

Geoffrey Archer—This former police detective's life was destroyed when his wife shot him and committed suicide after having been attacked by a serial rapist. Archer will do anything to stop the Lock Rapist—anything except unfreeze his heart.

Resa Wade—Her sister was attacked and raped by the Lock Rapist. The police say they've done all they can, but Resa isn't giving up. She wants the rapist behind bars—or dead. There's only one person who wants him more than she does, and that's Geoffrey Archer.

Earl Slattery—An installer of home security systems, Slattery has the perfect job. He can get past any lock, any alarm. When the one person who can identify him teams up with his nemesis, Geoffrey Archer, he must destroy them both or the burning inside him will never stop.

Clint Banes—Banes took over as lead detective on the Lock Rapist case after Archer was injured. But is Clint as dedicated to bringing the perp to justice as Archer?

Frank Berry—Archer's day manager of his basement firing range is a loyal friend. But associating with Archer could put his wife and himself in danger.

Prologue

The bright winter sun sent a pale rainbow of color through the sheer curtains.

The facets of a diamond solitaire sparkled with prisms of light, almost overpowering the hard blue glint that shone from the barrel of the 9mm Glock aimed at her head.

"No!" he cried. The breakfast tray in his hands tumbled slowly, silently to the floor as he dived toward the bed.

But no matter how fast he was, the bullet was faster. It happened as if in slow motion—her sad brown eyes meeting his, her hand turning—pointing the barrel of the gun at him, the tears glistening on her pale cheeks like the diamond on her left ring finger.

He reached out just as the gun's report echoed in his ears. The bullet stopped him in his tracks. Yet he still struggled to get to her, to somehow stop her. His bare feet slipped in juice, in coffee, in blood.

As he hit the bed and grabbed at her arm the second

shot rang out, and her blood spattered his face and hands, mingling with his own.

Geoffrey Archer opened his eyes to darkness and nauseating, aching loss. He kicked away the sweat-soaked sheets and vaulted up, crossing the room in two long strides. In the bathroom, he splashed cold water on his face, then leaned his forearms against the lavatory and hung his head, waiting for the nausea to pass.

Finally, he straightened, pushing his hair back with his hands. His right hand cramped, and burning pain shot through his fingers and up his wrist.

His legacy from his wife's suicide.

He massaged his wrist and flexed his fingers as he stepped to the window and threw back the drapes. The red and purple stain on the eastern sky reminded him of that last morning and his dream.

He'd been too slow. He was always too slow.

Chapter One

The barrel of the gun glinted blue in the bright lights. Theresa Wade stared at it, her fingers still chilled from touching the cold steel. She reached into her purse for a box of ammunition and set it down beside the gun. Then she set her purse aside and picked up the noise-canceling ear protectors.

After she'd donned the headgear and the safety goggles, she looked down the narrow corridor stretched out in front of her. At the far end, twenty-five yards away, was a piece of newsprint on which was printed the silhouette of a man's head and torso in deep blue.

There was no face on the silhouette, nor was there one in her mind. Still, she knew who the target represented. It was the shadowed face of the Lock Rapist. The man who'd raped her sister and five other women, the man she'd seen sneaking out of her apartment building that night. *The man who had seen her.*

With renewed determination, she looked down at

the gun. It didn't look like much lying there. A few inches of blue-black metal. A hollow tube with a handle.

She reached for the box of bullets, but her jaw clenched and her temples pounded. Her fingers closed in a fist.

"Come on, Resa," she whispered. *Pick it up.* She'd brought her gun in here. She'd set it on the counter. And if tonight went the way every other night had gone for the past two weeks, at the end of the evening she'd pick it up, slide it back into her purse alongside the box of bullets and leave the firing range.

But tonight wasn't like every other night.

Tonight she stopped waiting for Geoffrey Archer to come to her.

Frank Berry, the day manager of Archer's firing range outside of Nashville, had warned her, "You want to learn to handle that gun, come during the day. I'll be happy to teach you. But I leave at seven. After that, you're on your own."

She'd asked him about Archer.

"Yep. He's down here every evening till ten. But he's not gonna help you. Don't expect him to."

But she did. Archer was the reason she was here. She could feel him, sitting in his office near the stairs that led up from the basement firing range into the foyer of his Victorian home.

Detective Geoffrey Archer. *Former* detective with the Nashville Police Department.

She glanced at her watch. Ten minutes to ten. Every evening, right around this time, he came out of his office. He walked down the row of lanes—checking, she supposed, to see if everyone had left. Usually the only people who stayed this late were cops—both uniformed and detective, and her.

Tonight there was no one else here.

She flattened her palms against the counter and kept her eyes on the target as she took a careful breath and waited for him to walk by.

How did she know when he was behind her? Was it a scent? A change in the conditioned air that swirled around her? The ear protectors kept her from hearing his approach. Still, she knew that even if she could hear, she'd have to depend on her other senses. Because he moved as silently as a cat through his shadowy lair.

Something changed and a warm finger of awareness slid down her spine. He was there, behind her. Her shoulders tightened and she suppressed a shiver.

It had been six months since her sister's attack, but she still started at unexpected sounds and shied away from men. It had taken her weeks to step into an elevator if there was a man in it.

She took a deep breath and turned, but he was gone. *Damn him.* He'd done what he did every night. He'd paced the length of his massive basement, then slunk back to wherever he went—his office, his lair, his underground dungeon. She mentally shook her head at her silly thoughts.

Archer was no mysterious phantom, stealing through underground caverns, hiding from the light. He was just a man. A wounded, heartbroken man.

He and she had a lot in common, although he didn't know it. *Not yet.*

But he would find out tonight.

She removed the ear protectors and goggles and set them on the shelf, then stuffed the empty gun and ammunition into her purse.

She walked past the firing lanes toward the stairs. To her left was the table with the sign-in sheet for the range. To the right was his office. He was always in there sitting behind the desk when she came in. He'd never looked up.

Tonight she ignored the sign-in sheet. She turned and looked through the door into his office.

He was standing with his back to her, slowly and carefully writing something on a wall calendar. His white T-shirt stretched across his broad, spare shoulders and hung loosely over faded jeans that hugged his hips and butt in that way that only comes with years of wear and washing.

His body was long and lean, yet even with his back to her, he gave off a powerful presence that at once comforted and disturbed her.

He needed a haircut, but his just-too-long hair suited him. The wavy strands at the nape of his neck drew her eye. If she were interested in him—which she wasn't—she might be tempted to slide her fingers around his nape.

Just as she reminded herself that she only had one interest—learning to shoot her gun—his head angled like that of a predator sensing prey.

He turned and tossed the pen onto his desk, then raised his gaze to hers. His dark eyes were hooded, his brow furrowed. A few days' growth of beard shadowed his lean cheeks.

She fought not to lower her eyes. She'd felt his sharp gaze on her as he prowled the range, but nothing had prepared her for the impact of his eyes. Even though everything about him conveyed competence and protection, his piercing stare was grim and disapproving.

Resa lifted her chin and stared back. She would *not* be the first one to look away. She needed him, and she wasn't about to give him a reason to think she was a wimpy female.

A muscle in his jaw ticked. His mouth flattened into a frown and he crossed his arms.

"Can I help you?" he growled.

Resa's whole body went cold. She nearly turned and ran. But two things kept her rooted in place. Running was exactly what he wanted her to do. He wanted her to leave him alone. And she knew that if she didn't talk to him now she'd never get up the courage again.

Her jaw tightened. She sucked in courage with a deep breath. "I want you to help me."

She hadn't thought his eyes could get any darker, but they went as black and as opaque as coal.

"See Frank." He sat down in his desk chair and picked up a sheet of paper.

"I've seen Frank. He can't help me."

Archer put down the paper and stared at it for a few seconds. Then he leaned back in his chair and sent her a quelling glance. "If Frank can't help you, I sure can't."

"I'm paying a fee to rent a lane here." A couple of stray hairs tickled her eyelashes, but her hands were trembling too much and she didn't dare swipe them away.

Something flickered in his eyes. "Thank you," he said wryly as his dark gaze slid over her pale ecru blouse and sleek black trousers, not stopping until it settled on her überfashionable round-toed black pumps. Then he raised his brows and retraced each inch of her until he was looking into her eyes again.

His stare took her breath away. She swallowed. "I want you to teach me to shoot."

"No."

"No? What—why—" She was speechless. She'd expected him to give her a hard time, but he'd shot that single word at her like a bullet.

She closed her eyes for an instant, struggling to stay calm. She couldn't get rid of the urge to turn and run, and he knew it.

He was trying to intimidate her. *Trying,* ha. He'd succeeded, and he knew that too. But her sanity, maybe even her life, depended on persuading him to help her. She'd be damned if he would succeed in scaring her away.

When she opened her eyes he was watching her.

"Why not?" she asked. "This is a public range, isn't it?"

"Unfortunately."

"Well, *Detective* Archer, I'm paid through the end of the month."

He winced. "Geoffrey Archer. Not Detective."

His hostile growl rumbled through her. She'd thrown out his former title to try to gain a semblance of an advantage over him—and truthfully, to hit him where it hurt.

She'd definitely done that. Too well. She'd seen pain behind his narrowed eyes.

Involuntarily, she glanced down at his hands. They were big and elegant, with long blunt fingers. The only visible indication of the injury that had forced him to retire early was the network of scars across the back of his right hand, and the slight curve of his index finger.

She knew from newspaper reports that more than a year ago his wife had shot him in the hand before turning the gun on herself and committing suicide.

Feeling embarrassed that she'd deliberately baited him and unaccountably sorry for what had happened to him, Resa spun on her heel and walked back toward the lane she'd rented.

She stepped up to the counter and pulled the gun out of her purse. She ejected the empty magazine and laid it on the counter. Then she wrapped her fingers around the gun's handle.

She wasn't going to give up. She'd learn how to handle a gun. Eventually, she'd learn to shoot it, with or without Archer's help.

"What the hell are you doing?"

She jumped. He'd sneaked up on her, something she'd have thought he could never do. She answered him without turning around. "Learning to hold my weapon."

"It's nearly ten." His words were tight, squeezed out from his clenched jaw.

She felt a mean triumph. She'd forced him out from behind the barricade of his desk. She whirled and glared up at him. "I need a few more minutes."

Without meeting her gaze, he stalked away.

Gritting her teeth and ignoring the frustrated stinging behind her eyes, Resa awkwardly aimed her empty gun at the silhouette of the man who'd raped her sister.

ARCHER HEARD her high heels echoing across the concrete floor of the firing range. He tilted the desk chair back and glanced at his watch. 10:15 p.m. on the nose. Same time every night for the past two weeks. It was almost as if she stayed those extra minutes after closing time to taunt him.

Well, she taunted him all right. But not the way she intended to, he was sure.

She was persistent. And stubborn as hell. It seemed to him that she'd been here every night for at least a month.

He'd have to ask Frank when she'd originally signed up. Frank usually handled the billing and he'd warned Archer that she'd been coming during the day, but was planning to switch to evenings.

There were so many contradictions about her. She was obviously terrified of guns, yet she was determined to teach herself to use one. She did her best to project an image of calm assurance, but her dark-green eyes held a fear that she couldn't mask.

The bank of monitors on his office wall showed every accessible area of the range. He glanced up at the one connected to the camera at the top of the basement stairs. As she trudged up them, Archer saw the weariness etched in her face.

Quickly, he signed the last check and set down the pen. His hand ached. He rubbed his palm and then stretched his fingers, wincing as the tight muscles and newly reattached tendons resisted.

When he heard the door at the top of the stairs close, he stood and followed. At the top of the stairs, he flipped the light switch off. When he was fully cloaked in darkness, he opened the door and crossed the small foyer. He eased the front door open.

She was backing a white, late-model Sedan out of a parking space. He glanced at the dimly lit license plate—out of habit. He already knew her tag number. He'd watched her leave every night, just to make sure she got safely to her car.

She drove down the hill to the end of his driveway and turned right onto the farm road.

He stood there for a few seconds, then started to close the door. Just then he caught a flash through the brush, coming from where the driveway dead-ended into the road. He froze, stopping the door with his hand.

Within a few seconds, he saw another flash—the unmistakable reflection of the moon on metal. It was a car, running without lights. Following *her.*

"Damn," he whispered. "Who are you?"

For an instant he considered jumping into his own car and taking off after them. He considered calling her to warn her.

But it was none of his business. The flash could have been anything. A soup can on the side of the road. A puddle of water.

Hell, even if it were a car, for all he knew it was her boyfriend, making sure she got home safely.

"None of my business," he muttered as he locked the front door. He glanced to his right at the door that led to the main part of the house, but instead of locking up the firing range and heading to the kitchen to find something to eat, he pushed open the door labeled Firing Range and took the stairs back down to the basement.

The daily sign-in book was beside the entrance at the bottom of the stairs. The last line read, Resa Wade: in 8:03 p.m., out 10:15 p.m.

He flipped the pages backward.

Resa Wade: in 8:02 p.m., out 10:12 p.m.
Resa Wade: in 8:00 p.m., out 10:14 p.m.

His detective's brain catalogued the information and categorized her. She was honest. Careful. Detail-oriented.

And familiar. At least her name was. He knew he'd never met her before she'd come to his range. He'd have remembered that creamy skin, those dark-green eyes, that sun-shot brown hair.

And that attitude. His mouth almost curved into a smile before he stopped it. Frowning, he headed for his office. There were only two reasons for him to be so certain he knew her. The first could be eliminated out of hand. He hadn't been with a woman since his wife had died more than a year ago. In fact, he'd hardly seen a woman in all that time, until Resa Wade showed up.

So the reason he found her name familiar had to be reason number two. He went into his office and sat down at the desk. Locked in the bottom drawer was a thick file folder containing all the information he'd gathered over the past three years on the Lock Rapist—the monster who'd caused his wife's death— who'd taken away the only two things that had ever mattered to him. His wife and his career.

With a gun hand that didn't work, he'd had no choice but to take a disability pension. They'd offered him a desk job, but there was no way he could be chained to a desk for the next fifteen years. The forced retirement was marginally less humiliating than answering phones and doing computer searches while enduring his fellow officers' pity.

He pulled his key ring from his pocket and unlocked the drawer. Using his left hand, he lifted the heavy folder out.

An icy chill of dread snaked down his spine as he opened the file. This had to be how he knew Resa Wade.

She was somehow connected to the Lock Rapist.

RESA WAS almost home. She glanced at the dashboard clock. Ten forty-five. A huge sigh escaped her lips. She was so tired. It was a bone-deep weariness that came from too much stress and too little sleep.

She'd been to Archer's firing range every single night for the past two weeks, ever since she'd come back from Louisville, Kentucky.

That last trip to her mother's home was her seventh in the six months since Celia had been attacked. Her mother wanted her to move to Louisville and help with her sister. Celia wasn't doing well. She couldn't sleep despite tranquilizers and sleeping pills. She sat in the living room looking out the picture window and chain-smoking. She wouldn't wash her hair or eat unless someone was there to coax her.

Resa's mother was at the end of her rope, and so was Resa. She'd offered to pay for Celia to go to a psychiatric facility, but her mom wouldn't hear of that.

So Resa had told her there was nothing else she could do. She'd been away from her work too long, and her work was in Nashville. Her stress level wasn't helped by her guilt over leaving her mother to deal with Celia.

She lifted her hair off her neck. A dull pounding headache reverberated through her skull. She was exhausted, and yet she felt jittery. It would be another long night without sleep. And tomorrow, she had two fittings and a consultation.

A country-music award ceremony was coming up in August. Her most important challenge yet. She was designing outfits for two of the nominees and a performer. She had to get some sleep. She couldn't afford to screw up her biggest chance at exposure for her clothing designs.

She turned onto Valley Street, headed toward her new apartment. As she straightened the wheel, she glanced in the rearview mirror. A dark sedan had turned behind her, about three car lengths back.

She examined the shape of the headlights and the grille. It looked like the same car she'd spotted following her last week—last Tuesday to be precise.

Just like last week, she had no idea where she'd picked him up. She hadn't noticed anyone behind her, then suddenly there he was. It had to be him. The Lock Rapist. Who else would follow her?

Despite the warm May night, her palms grew clammy and cold. Fear skittered up her spine. She reached over and dug the Glock out of her purse, a futile gesture. Even if she were able to load it, she'd never get off a shot in time to save her life. Her only hope was that maybe if he saw the gun, it would scare him.

The idea that the same man who'd brutally attacked her sister and five other innocent women was following her sent terror arrowing through her chest. But why would he follow her? And how had he found her? She'd moved and changed her phone number and her e-mail address.

Her face might be familiar. After all, she'd been interviewed several times about her sister's attack. But she'd told all the reporters that she hadn't gotten a good look at the face of the man she'd seen running from her apartment building.

She looked in the rearview mirror again without angling her head.

If it was he, what was he waiting for? Why hadn't he made a move? He could grab her at any time. He could break into her apartment while she slept. That was what he'd done with the other women.

Celia had been asleep in Resa's second bedroom. She hadn't heard anything. Hadn't known anything was wrong until a musty cloth covered her face. At that point, Celia's account of the attack became sketchy and disjointed. Resa figured it was just as well if she didn't remember the specifics.

The back of her neck prickled. She felt his eyes on her as the car inched closer—closer. She fought the urge to hunch her shoulders. She was gripping the steering wheel so tightly her hands cramped.

"Come on, you monster," she whispered through clenched teeth. "Do something. Just give me one good look at you." She glanced in her driver's-side mirror. "Come a little bit closer."

She squinted, trying to make out the letters and numbers on the front license plate. But the suburban street was too dark.

After she'd seen the car last Tuesday, she'd called the police and spoken to the detective who'd handled Celia's case.

Detective Clint Banes had been polite and concerned about her fear that she was being followed, but he'd been careful not to give her false hope. He didn't have enough manpower to put a twenty-four-hour watch on her, he'd said. Not even enough for a night watch.

You've got to be careful, he told her. *Don't go out alone. Get his license plates. Or at least the make of the car. If it is the Lock Rapist, and we can ID him through his vehicle, we can find the evidence to put him away.*

He offered her the chance to come in and view photos of cars to try and pick out which one was following her. She'd thanked him and hung up.

She turned at the entrance to the gated community where she now lived, apprehension squeezing her chest. She had to stop a few feet ahead to swipe her entry card. She reached up and made sure her car doors were locked.

What would he do? Last week he'd turned just as she approached the well-lit apartment complex. Was he bolder this week? What would she do if he pulled in behind her?

If he did follow her up to the gate, she'd be able to see the color of his car, maybe even get his license plate.

But she'd also be vulnerable. The few seconds before the gates opened were plenty of time for him to jump out of his car and grab her.

She pulled up to the card reader, her card ready, and glanced in the mirror.

The dark sedan slowed down then continued on without turning. He drove under a streetlight, but the light's glow wasn't bright enough to give her a clue about whether the vehicle was black or dark blue or some other color.

At least he'd given up for the moment—or gotten tired—or received a cell phone call. Whatever the reason, he was gone for now.

Hardly daring to breathe, she swiped her entry card through the slot, keeping an eye out behind her. As soon as the gates began to swing open, she pulled forward.

The gates closed silently behind her. She was safe.

A shiver racked her body. Quickly, jerkily, she pulled into her parking place and ran up the stairs to her apartment.

As she closed and locked the door behind her, the feeling of safety dissolved into fear as her brain replayed what had just happened.

Her hands flew to her mouth as her throat closed up, threatening to cut off her breath.

She wasn't safe. The Lock Rapist knew where she lived.

EARL SLATTERY quietly unlocked the door of the modest clapboard house. He sneaked in, eased the door closed and put on the chain. So far, so good.

He'd had a profitable evening. He'd found out where Theresa Wade lived. With a little judicious sneaking around he'd discovered a breach in the fence on the back side of her apartment complex. He had all the information he needed.

Now if he could just make it upstairs to bed without his wife waking up—

Bright lights blinded him. He jerked violently and whirled.

"Earl, where have you been?"

He cringed at his wife's strident tone. He'd have thought he'd be used to it after twenty years of marriage. *But no.* It still shredded his nerves like a cheese grater.

"Hi, honey," he said, giving her an innocent smile. "I told you I'd be working late tonight."

"You install security systems. It's after eleven. You expect me to believe you've been wiring somebody's windows and doors all this time—in the dark?"

Earl went over to her and pressed a kiss to her damp forehead. "I do what my boss tells me to do, sweetheart—"

"You do what *I* tell you to do. And don't feed me that sweetheart crap. I'm sick of your whining and I'm sick of your lies. Don't forget my promise. If I ever find out you're cheating on me I'll cut off your—"

"Mom—I'm thirsty!"

"Well, at least you're home. See if you can shut those kids up, will you?"

"Sure thing, sweetheart. And maybe after I take a shower, we can—" he waggled his eyebrows at her.

She cowed him with a disgusted look. "This time of night? Get home on time to help me with the kids tomorrow and we'll see. Meantime, you need to get up in the morning and get the kids off to school. I'll be too tired."

Earl escaped upstairs, nearly tripping on a toy car on the floor in the hall. He fetched his youngest son a drink of water and told all three children to settle down and go to sleep. He stood at the door and watched the three of them bedded down in the same room.

"Someday," he whispered. "Someday we'll have a great big house. Each one of you will have your own room, with your own TV." Things he'd never had living with his grandpa after his mom was murdered.

He stepped into his bedroom and stopped cold. On the floor in front of the closet was his wife's old hard-sided suitcase. His heart jumped into his throat. That meant only one thing.

It was time! She was leaving!

Thank goodness! The flame inside him had been building. Day by day it grew until his insides sizzled with the heat. He shook his head and licked his lips. It seemed as if the burning started sooner and built faster these days. He was having trouble controlling it for six long months between Mary Nell's visits to her mother.

If he were lucky, maybe they'd leave before the weekend. As soon as she and the kids were out of the house, he could begin to prepare.

He took out his wallet and extracted the tiny worn envelope from a secret pocket. For an instant he looked at the faded postmark and the almost unreadable address on the front of the envelope. Mrs. Hannah Slattery. His mom.

He touched the name, then peeked inside. There was the lock of honey-blond hair. And beside it the few precious golden strands that remained of his mom's hair. He brought the envelope to his nose and inhaled.

He loved the smell of freshly-washed hair—blond and soft like Mom's. He squirmed and tugged at his pants. Damn that woman of his. He needed some relief.

Carefully, he tucked the envelope back in his wallet. Soon he'd be able to replace the lock of hair. Then he'd be okay for a few more months.

He headed for the shower. It angered him that his wife turned her nose up at him. In the whole time they'd been married, she'd never done anything when he wanted to. It was always her timetable. Sometimes he wondered what she'd do if he used her to ease the inferno building inside him.

He immediately wiped those thoughts out of his head. She was his wife. The mother of his children. He could never do that to her.

He held his face up to the shower spray, reliving the fragrance of his mom's hair, and the girl's. The smell renewed him and cooled the burning, at least for a while.

Mary Nell and the kids would leave in a few days. Then he'd be on his own for at least a week, maybe more. He could hold out that long.

Chapter Two

By the time Resa Wade showed up at the firing range the next night, Archer knew a lot more about her than he wanted to. He'd spent most of the previous night poring over the thick file in his desk drawer. It contained copies of the police reports for each of the Lock Rapist's attacks.

Then, after a couple of hours' restless sleep, he'd called his former partner, who'd taken over the case after Archer was injured.

Clint had verified what he'd already figured out. Theresa Wade was sister to the Lock Rapist's sixth victim, Celia Ramsey. Celia had been separated from her husband and staying with Resa when the attack occurred.

He asked Clint what he thought about Resa.

"I don't know," Clint had answered. "She's pretty, like her sister. Why?"

"She's been here every night for the past two weeks."

"Here? Where? You mean at your house?" Clint's voice rose in disbelief.

"At the range."

"Oh." Clint took a deep breath. "She called me about a week ago. Said she was being followed. Said she was sure it was the Lock Rapist."

"What?" It was Archer's turn to be surprised—and furious. "Why didn't you tell me?"

Clint hesitated for a beat. "You're not on the case, Geoff."

"I've got a stake in it!"

"I know you do."

"You think it's him? How would he know about her?"

"I don't know if he's following her or if she's just nervous after her sister's attack. But she's *kind of* an eyewitness."

Archer slammed his fist down on the desk. "What the hell is kind of an eyewitness?"

"She saw the Lock Rapist running from the scene that night."

"Damn it, Clint. You promised you'd keep me in the loop."

"Geoff, you need to get past this. You chose to leave the force."

He flexed his fingers, flinching when they ached. "Some choice. Sit behind a desk or retire."

Clint was silent.

"So are you censoring what you think I can handle and what I can't? You don't get to do that."

"Actually I do. I'm already skating pretty close to busting regulations by copying reports and depositions for you."

Clint was right. He wasn't obligated to tell Archer anything about the case. Archer was no longer a cop.

"Have you at least got a car tailing her?"

"Can't afford it. Crime is up twenty percent in our precinct and the governor wants to keep up with surrounding states that are enacting no-tolerance policies for conviction. I told her to get his license-plate number and let me know."

"Get his license— Clint, you know as well as I do that it's him. If you don't give her some protection, she's a sitting duck." He winced at the harsh words, knowing they were true.

"I wish I could. The budget's worse than it was last year."

"This might be your big chance to break the case. He follows her here. I saw a reflection from a car last night. He was waiting for her at the end of my driveway."

"You were watching her drive away?"

"It was kind of late. I just wanted to make sure everything was okay. After I saw that I thought about following her."

"Why didn't you?"

Archer's shoulders lifted involuntarily in a shrug. "For all I knew it could have been her boyfriend. It could have been a car passing on the road, although that doesn't happen very often out here. Besides, it's none of my business."

The words hung between them for a few seconds.

"None of your business. I see. So why'd you call me? Just to hassle me?"

Archer clamped his jaw shut. What could he say? He couldn't tell Clint how Resa's determination and naive bravery tugged at his sore heart. "You're going to have another rape. You know that."

Clint didn't respond.

"And maybe even a murder, if the Lock Rapist thinks Resa can ID him."

"Off the record—if I were you, I'd make sure she knows how to shoot to kill."

Archer planned to do just that. He'd tamped down his anger and frustration and asked Clint to fax him Resa's statement and any other pertinent information he was missing.

Now he looked down at the statement Resa had given police on the night of her sister's rape. She'd reported seeing a slight, medium-height figure in a dark hoodie running from her apartment building as she entered that night. She'd wondered about him, but figured he could be anybody from a spooked would-be burglar to a college student out for a late jog. So she'd gone on up to her apartment, where she discovered the door unlocked and her sister collapsed on the floor.

Archer shuffled the papers Clint had faxed to him, but nothing else stood out, except that the follow-up of her statement had been perfunctory.

After making sure the files were locked in his bottom desk drawer, Archer stepped out of his office and looked down the long corridor of firing lanes set up for shooting practice.

A pair of street cops from the 10th were just wrapping up. He made small talk with them for a couple of minutes before they took off. Once they were gone he walked down to lane fourteen and stopped at the edge of the free-standing cubicle.

Resa stood behind the counter with goggles and noise-canceling ear protectors on. She held the gun in one shaky hand.

She wore a frilly blouse and a dark-green straight skirt that strained over her bottom and hugged her hips as she stood balanced with her legs apart.

For a minute, he just watched her. In heels, she was about three inches shorter than he. Her legs were long and curvy, her bottom was shapely and her blouse outlined the delicately toned muscles in her back and shoulders. Her hair was a sort of medium brown— nothing special, except that under the harsh fluorescent lights it shimmered with dozens of unnamable colors.

As he watched, she dropped her gun hand to the counter and uttered a sigh.

Anger, swift and hot, rushed through him. The pressure had been building all day, ever since he'd talked to Clint. He was angry at her for coming here, angry at Clint for dismissing the danger to her, and angry at himself for not nailing the bastard who'd followed her.

But mostly he was furious with her. He knew what she was doing. He'd seen it in victims and their loved ones. She wanted to learn how to shoot so she could take out the man who'd attacked her sister.

Despite what Clint had said, and his initial agreement, he'd decided that arming her against the unknown predator was a stupid plan. It was more likely to get her killed than to protect her.

But he knew how she felt. For months after his wife's death, he'd dreamed one dream. In it he tracked down the monster who had killed Natalie as surely as if he'd fired the gun himself.

And every time Archer found him, he held his police-issue SIG 220 in his right hand and pulled the trigger—once, twice, three times, until blood coated everything and he was sure the bastard was dead.

But that was just a dream. He no longer had the luxury of shooting with his right hand. The bullet Natalie had shot at him had severed three tendons and made mincemeat out of the nerves running to his trigger finger.

He couldn't shoot worth a damn with his left hand, and Resa knew nothing at all about guns or shooting. Neither one of them would ever make good on their dream of stopping the Lock Rapist.

She left the gun on the counter and flexed her fingers. Just as he was about to tap her shoulder, she went still.

She realized he was there. She turned, removing the ear protectors and sent him a narrow glance.

"What do you think you're doing with that gun?" he growled.

Her dark-green eyes flashed. "Learning how to shoot it, Detective."

He blew out an exasperated breath. "You'll never learn like that," he growled through clenched teeth. "And I told you I'm not a detective. Call me Geoff, or Archer."

Something dark and soft flickered in her green eyes for an instant. "Sorry. I'll be more careful, Mr. Archer."

Mr. Archer. Was she deliberately trying to rile him? If so, she was doing a damn good job of it.

"I thought you were going to come back during the day and see Frank."

"That was your idea. I told you Frank can't help me with what I want."

"All right, I'll bite. What *do* you want?"

Her gaze faltered. She looked down at her fingers. "I want you to teach me how to protect myself."

His jaw ached from clenching. He ought to turn on his heel right now. He sure as hell shouldn't keep talking to her. "Protect yourself from whom? And why me?"

She opened her mouth, then closed it. Closed her eyes briefly, then opened them. Suddenly she looked tired and small and vulnerable.

He steeled himself against the feeling that he should be nicer to her. *Nice* wasn't going to keep her from doing something stupid. *Nice* wouldn't keep her safe.

He'd had enough. Time to stop dancing around the truth. "I know who you are."

Her back stiffened. "Do you?"

"Yes, I do. And I know that there's a firing range about four miles from your brand-new apartment complex. So why did you come all the way out here to Cheatham County—three times that distance, to stand in a firing lane and stare at your empty gun?"

She shrugged, but her effort to appear nonchalant failed. "I heard about your range—"

He cut her off. "No, you didn't. I don't advertise. I don't give lessons."

"But you *are* open to the public."

"Unfortunately." His accountant had recommended that he make the range available to the public. He couldn't afford to maintain the house just on his pension and his teaching salary. "But this range is primarily for my personal use and for the use of the Nashville P.D."

She shrugged. "Well, your day manager, Frank, took my money quickly enough and assigned me a firing lane. You let me know if I'm taking up valuable space that your police buddies could be using." She started to turn back to the range, but he caught her arm.

"You came here because of me, didn't you?" He glared at her.

Resa swallowed and tried to look innocent. She hadn't realized it herself at first. She'd convinced herself that she needed her days free for designing, sewing and client fittings.

She'd made friends with Frank, and through their conversations she'd found out that Archer spent his mornings at Tennessee State University where he taught two graduate courses in Criminal Justice. Then he drove to Vanderbilt Medical Center for two hours a day of physical therapy on his hand.

It had taken her a few days to admit to herself that she'd changed to evenings so she could see him.

All those thoughts rushed through her head in the few seconds while Archer took a deep breath.

"Don't give me that wide-eyed look," he said. "If you think I'm going to help you because we've both been affected by the Lock Rapist, you can get that out of your head right now."

"Affected?" She stared at him. "Mr. Archer, people are *affected* by a sad movie or an unexpected compliment."

Archer felt pinned by her dark-green eyes. "What do you want me to say? That he ripped our lives to shreds?" The words rasped in his throat. "Okay. I'll give you that."

She glanced down at his right hand, which was aching with the effort to hold on to her arm. When she looked back up, he saw that same soft, dark flicker in her eyes that he'd seen before. He jerked his hand away.

"You haven't told me why you came here. Why me?"

"If you know who I am, then you know why I'm here." She wrapped her arms around herself and looked at a point beyond his shoulder. "My sister left her husband in June of last year. She'd had enough of his drinking and violence. She came to stay with me to—as she put it—absorb some of my strength." She laughed shortly. "If she only knew."

He waited.

"Anyhow, she was doing really well. By December, she'd decided to file for divorce. But—"

"But she was attacked."

She nodded, looking down. Her fingertips whitened as she tightened her grip on her arms. "It destroyed her. She was never strong—" Resa raised her gaze to his. "She depended on me to keep her safe. And I didn't."

Pain sliced through Archer's chest. *She depended on me.* How many times had he thought the same thing? Resa's sister sounded a lot like his wife. Fragile. Fearful. She'd depended on him to protect her. And he'd failed.

He and Resa were more alike than he'd realized. And he hated it. He didn't want to be like her. He sure as hell didn't want to know how she felt, or recognize how badly she hurt.

Resolutely, he pushed his own pain and regret back where it belonged, in the lockbox where he kept his heart. "So what now? You're going to become a one-woman vigilante force and go after the guy the Nashville P.D. hasn't been able to catch in three years?"

Her face turned bright pink, but she lifted her chin and met his gaze. "I want to learn how to protect myself."

Archer felt something break inside him. He tried to ignore it, but it was too late. The box around his heart had developed a crack, and compassion was leaking out and taunting him with his failure.

He hadn't been able to save his wife. Hadn't been able to stop the attacks. Could he leave Resa alone to face the monster who'd destroyed both their lives? He knew he couldn't.

"Put your ear protectors on," he said. He dug in his jeans' pocket for a pair of earplugs and stuck them in his ears. "Can you hear me?"

She nodded. "Barely."

"Good. Pick up the gun."

Her head turned toward him. "You're going to teach me? I thought you said—"

He shrugged. "I'd have a mess to clean up if you blew off your toe, or someone else's."

He heard a quiet huff. It almost made him smile.

She picked up the Glock 19 9mm. It was a compact gun, ideal for carrying as a concealed weapon.

"First thing—every time you pick up your weapon, check to see if it's loaded." His voice cracked. Self-loathing blanketed him. He knew better than to leave his gun loaded. Knew better than to leave it in plain view on his dresser. But it was too late now.

"It's loaded," Resa said. "I loaded it a little while ago. For the first time."

"Check it. Check it every single time. Do you know how to eject the magazine?"

She pressed the release and the magazine dropped into her left hand.

"Now inspect it. Make sure the rounds are straight and ready to feed."

"What if I'm being attacked or carjacked? I can't tell the guy 'Hang on while I check my weapon.'"

"This is basic maintenance. You check it twice a day. And once a week, you clean it, whether you've fired it or not."

She glanced at the top of the magazine and ran her thumb across the bullets. She had sixteen rounds. Archer would bet money she wouldn't get a single shot off if she were in a desperate situation. "Good. Slap the magazine back into place."

She followed his instructions, her hands shaking a little.

"It's okay. You're doing great," he murmured. "Now, rest your right hand in your left palm."

She complied clumsily. "I don't know about this. It feels awkward. Can you show me how?"

He grimaced. He could, but it would be hard, in more ways than one. Even after spending months in physical therapy, and doing strengthening reps on his own, he still had trouble grasping anything heavier than a wine bottle. His buddies on the force, with the exception of Clint, didn't know how bad the damage to his hand was.

But there was a second problem. It had been months since he'd talked to anyone other than Frank or Clint or his students. He'd had his basement enlarged into an indoor range so he could practice shooting. But after Natalie's funeral and his surgeries, the cavernous below-ground range appealed to his need to hide out and lick his wounds. He'd forgotten how to talk to people.

So, whether he tried to shoot the gun himself or got close enough to her to show her how, he'd be revealing his weakness to her. He weighed his two options and decided he'd rather touch her than the gun. He was too proud and stubborn to risk dropping it in front of her.

He took a step forward and reached around her, which placed her back and bottom firmly against him. She stiffened slightly. To his surprise his body stirred to life.

He hadn't felt anything in so long. Not lust, or curiosity, or even much pain. After Natalie had shot him and killed herself, he'd cut off the last of his emotions.

The idea that he could react to a woman's body dismayed him. It felt like a betrayal of his wife. He swallowed.

Even though his arms were longer than Resa's, the tiny cubicle made it difficult to move away from the warm firmness of her body. Not to mention that his nose was practically buried in her hair. It was soft and smooth, and smelled like summer, like melons and sunshine.

He clenched his jaw and concentrated on showing her how to hold the squarish, chunky little Glock.

He pressed the grip against her right palm. "Wrap your thumb and these three fingers around the handle, and your index finger on the trigger."

Then he showed her how to rest her right hand in the palm of her left. Her hands were cold. He could feel her trembling. Was it because she was afraid of the gun? Or of him?

"There. That's how you should hold a gun. No one-handed gunslinging. No ridiculous sideways shots like you see in movies. Hold it gently but firmly in both hands." He bent his head toward her ear. "And relax. You're too stiff."

Okay, that was close. He let go of her and leaned against the bulletproof wall. He sighed, hoping to expel the scent of her hair from his nostrils. He forced himself to concentrate on her hands. She was the first woman he'd even looked at since his wife had died. And he wasn't happy about it.

"Now line the sights up with your right eye," he ordered gruffly. "No, don't close the left one. Keep them both open. Aim for his chest."

She uttered a little moan and the barrel wavered.

"Come on, Resa. You said you wanted to protect yourself. Well, this is how you do it. If you're going to handle a gun, you've got to master it. You're in charge. You—not the gun. Now grip it like I showed you."

Her shoulders squared and her chin rose. Her fingers tightened around the gun.

"Look at the target. That's a dangerous man."

"The Lock Rapist," she whispered.

"If you had to, could you shoot him?" He saw her throat move as she swallowed.

"Resa," he snapped. "Could you shoot him?"

"Yes." Her voice was shaky. "I think so."

"Because if you don't *know* you could pull the trigger, we'll stop right now. If you aren't ready to defend yourself with deadly force, you'll just end up putting yourself in more danger."

She took a deep breath and a round bit of creamy flesh swelled above the low neckline of her top.

"I can do it." This time her voice was stronger.

"Good." He forced his attention back to the gun.

"Now, when I say so, squeeze the trigger smoothly. Don't jerk, don't hesitate. Just squeeze."

She raised the gun a bit and sighted down it as she took another long breath.

Archer breathed with her, unable to take his eyes off her strong, delicately rounded arms. He watched, fascinated, as her index finger tightened on the trigger, just like he'd told her.

The gun went off.

Resa had expected the gun to kick, but it still surprised her.

"Oh!" Her heart pounded. Her fingers tingled with reaction from the gun's report.

Archer stood behind and to the left of her, so close she could feel his breaths on her neck. So close she could smell his clean, citrus scent.

"That was good. Very smooth."

"Smooth? Really? I thought I was going to drop it. I'm not sure I could do it again. I didn't expect the trigger to be that hard to pull." Her voice was as shaky as the rest of her.

"Glocks don't have a safety. You can adjust the trigger sensitivity but I wouldn't recommend it."

She took off the headphones and let them rest around her neck. Leaning forward, she squinted at the target. "How do you think I did?"

"On your first shot? There's a small chance you hit the target."

His voice sounded amused, but when she glanced up there was no trace of a smile on his hard, classically molded face. Instead, he frowned and turned his attention to the recall button. Was he embarrassed by his joke? Or by the fact that he'd been lured into small talk? His cheeks seemed pinker than they had been.

The target swayed in the breeze it created as it floated toward them. She didn't see a hole.

"I missed the whole thing." Her ears burned with chagrin.

The target came to a stop in front of the counter.

"No, you didn't. Look right there." Archer pointed at the lower left of the silhouette. "You got him in the kidneys."

"I was aiming for his *heart,*" she said harshly. The silhouette was the rapist, and right then she wanted him to die for what he'd done to her sister.

Archer's black eyelashes floated down and back up, and he sent her a searching look. Then he nodded.

"Shoot again. This time get off three shots as fast as you can." He sent the target back downrange.

She fired, then she put the gun down as if it had

burned her. "That's all." She held out her hands, splaying the fingers. "I'm too shaky, and I closed my eyes on the last shot."

He took her hands in his and turned them palm up. "You might want to wear gloves for a while—driving gloves so your fingers aren't covered, until your skin toughens up." He touched a red place on her palm. "You could get blisters."

His warm hands bothered her. She didn't like the way his touch made her feel—cared for, protected. She knew from long experience that she couldn't trust that feeling. She'd never been able to depend on others to take care of her. Her mother had worked two jobs and juggled a string of boyfriends. With teaching during the day and waitressing at night, she'd never had time for Resa and her sister, so Resa had raised Celia. And of course it was Resa that Celia had come to when she left her deadbeat jerk of a husband.

She pulled her hands away from Archer's touch.

"So what's your plan, Resa?"

His question caught her off guard. "My plan? Oh, you mean for the gun?" She swallowed and prepared to lie. "After what happened to my sister, I just think I'll feel better knowing I have protection."

"You're not fooling me, you know."

She took off the headphones and set them on the shelf, then picked up the gun and ejected the magazine. "Fooling you? I'm not trying to fool you."

"You saw him."

The blunt words shocked her. She dropped the

magazine to the countertop. "I saw—I saw someone. I have no idea if it was him or not. How could I know?"

"You're the only witness they have, other than the victims. And they all swear he threw something over their faces so they couldn't see anything. They could be lying—out of fear, maybe, but so far we haven't been able to crack them."

"I knew Celia couldn't give a description. But none of the others could, either?"

He shook his head. "They were all attacked in the dark. All asleep. None of them heard anything before he covered their faces. So you're the only person who can possibly identify him. And he saw you."

Again, his words, uttered in that low, deep voice, ripped through her like a bullet. "He turned and looked at me. He had on a hooded jacket. His face was shadowed. I couldn't see anything but his eyes, and I'm not completely sure that I saw them. I *felt* them."

She shuddered and took a step toward him. She had to get out of the tiny cubicle. It suddenly felt too small, too hot. "Excuse me."

Archer didn't move. "Not yet." He put a hand on either wall. With his height and his broad shoulders, he loomed over her. The fact that he was so much bigger and stronger than her and was blocking her way should have alarmed her, but oddly she felt safe, protected.

"Do you know the person who's following you?"

"Following me? How—" Her throat closed up. She

hadn't told anyone except the police detective about the dark sedan. It took her a moment to get her voice back. "How do you know that?"

"I saw a car pull out behind you last night."

"You did?" A small shred of hope dangled in front of her like a carrot. Maybe if he thought she was in danger, he would help her after all. "You were watching?"

"This house is on a hill. I could see the moon glinting off a metal surface. Then after you turned, it moved. It wasn't somebody you know?"

She shook her head. "It's him. I can feel it. It's like he's toying with me. If I slow down, he slows down with me. If I try to maneuver under a streetlight so I can see the make of his car or get a glimpse of the front plate, he hangs back or turns." She shuddered. "Last night he followed me all the way to my apartment complex."

Archer pinned her with his glare. "You *knew* he was behind you and you led him to your apartment?"

"I live in a gated community."

He cursed. "That only works if you're *behind* the gate."

"The gatehouse is well-lit. He turned away when I pulled up to the gate. What else could I have done?"

"You could have turned around and come back here. You could have called the police." He massaged his right palm.

"Right. I called Detective Banes last week. Fat lot of good it did."

"So now the Lock Rapist knows where you live."

She nodded miserably.

"Okay. Get out your cell phone. I want to give you my number and get yours."

She retrieved her cell phone from her purse and entered his number.

"Now. You should move—immediately. And hire a security service."

"I just moved *there*. It was the only gated complex in Nashville that I could afford, and I can barely pay the rent now. There's no way I can move again. And I'd never manage to pay a private security firm." She managed a small smile. "So it looks like I'm on my own. Now can I leave?"

His brow furrowed and he studied her with those dark eyes. She stepped forward, violating his comfort zone and her own. She felt heat radiating from him through the barriers of their clothes. It had to be her imagination.

He lowered his arms and stood aside, giving her a free path out of the lane.

"I'll follow you home tonight."

She turned to look at him. "What? No. I can't let you do that. I'm fine—besides…"

He watched her expectantly.

She swallowed. "You're going to think I'm crazy."

A tight smile lit his face. "I doubt it. Hell, most days I feel like I'm going nuts myself."

"I think he only follows me on Tuesday. But then I've only noticed him twice, so that's hardly a representative sample."

"No, but it could be significant. The attacks have occurred in a regular pattern too. June and December, with one exception." Bitterness edged his voice.

She considered his words. "My sister's attack was this past December. When exactly were the others?"

"December two years ago, then the next June, then December again—" he paused for an instant "—then February, June, and your sister this past December."

February. The one anomaly in the rapist's pattern. Archer's wife's attack. "And you were on the case for—?"

"I took over as lead detective after the second rape." He wiped his face. The pale web of scars on the back of his hand glimmered in the harsh range lights. "The first thing I did was cut off all media attention. He wasn't happy about that."

"Media attention? Why would he want attention?" Resa asked.

"Serial offenders typically crave the notoriety. Plus, they *need* to gloat over how far behind the investigators are. They'll go to almost any lengths to keep the media's attention focused on them."

Resa's stomach churned with a sudden relization. "Oh, Archer. That's why he attacked your wife," she whispered.

He nodded shortly, and Resa saw his jaw muscles tense. "This guy is obviously very organized. Maybe not by choice. His job could force him into a pattern. Or it could be his home situation. He may have a family—"

Resa gasped. "A family? That can't be possible. How could a man with a wife and children do the things he does?"

Archer turned off a bank of lights, throwing the firing range into darkness. His office and the entrance to the stairs were the only lighted areas. "Many serial offenders have families. If you were to look in on them at home, they'd seem like ordinary working stiffs. He might even coach Little League."

"Oh my God." She'd thought of the Lock Rapist as a shadowy entity who emerged to attack his victims, then faded back into some dark abyss until his next attack.

She'd never considered the possibility that he had a life.

"How can someone who has a family—a wife—" her voice choked.

Archer shook his head. "There are certain common predictors of deviant behavior or violence. But nothing's ever that easy. No one knows why one man crosses the line and another doesn't." He stepped into his office and grabbed a set of keys from his desktop. "Are you ready?"

"You don't have to follow me home. Like I told you, I've only noticed him on Tuesdays." The idea that the man who'd attacked her sister had placed following her on his regular schedule spooked her.

Tuesday: pick up milk, call the plumber, follow Theresa Wade.

An icy chill slid down her spine and she shuddered.

Archer turned out the lights in his office, then placed a guiding hand on the small of her back. "Let's go."

Resa opened her mouth to protest again, but Archer's warm protective touch at the small of her back made her feel safer than she'd felt in months, maybe ever.

On the other hand, his certainty that she needed protection increased the cold fear that had haunted her ever since her sister's attack.

The Lock Rapist thought she could recognize him. He considered her a threat. And when he caught her, he'd kill her.

Chapter Three

The following Tuesday Earl Slattery got out of the shower and grabbed two towels. Mary Nell didn't like for him to use two—wasteful, she said.

But tonight was special. He scrubbed his wet hair with one and wrapped the other around his waist. Then he grinned at himself in the mirror.

He'd suggested to his boss that having one night a week set aside for evening installations and repair of security equipment would increase business. His boss had gone for it, so Earl had volunteered for late shift on Tuesdays.

It was perfect. Especially now that he'd picked up the scent of the woman he'd seen that night. If he busted his butt to finish by nine o'clock on Tuesday nights, he had plenty of time to follow Theresa home.

After her initial suspicion, Mary Nell had gotten used to his late hours on Tuesdays. That sure made it easier on him. As long as he was careful and got his installations done in plenty of time, he could do anything he wanted.

It bothered him that Theresa Wade was going to Detective Archer's gun range. He'd considered going in there himself, to see if she was shooting or if she and Archer had a thing going.

But that was high risk, and Earl avoided as many high-risk behaviors as he could.

Last Tuesday night, he'd discovered a way to slip inside the fence that surrounded Theresa's gated community, so earlier tonight he'd sneaked in, bypassed the security system in a matter of seconds, and entered her apartment. He'd slipped a note under the edge of her windowsill, as if it had been slid under from outside. Then he'd driven out to Detective Archer's house, waited until he and Theresa left, and stuck the second note in Archer's mailbox.

That had been exciting. Much more exciting than following Theresa's car. More danger. More adrenaline. But not really more risk.

He liked that. All this sneaking around gave him a nearly fail-safe way to experience the excitement without risking so much.

Slinging the towel around his neck, Earl closed his eyes. Tonight's excitement had almost dulled the burning for a little while.

And tomorrow... He couldn't wait for tomorrow to get here. The kids had been out of school for a week, but Mary Nell had delayed her trip because the car needed a tune-up. Tomorrow morning she and the kids were heading up to Knoxville, to her mother's.

It was time. Earl shuddered in anticipation. Soon he could feed the hungry monster that lurked inside him and the burning would ease—for a while. He smacked his lips, then picked up his comb.

"Earl!"

Grimacing, he quickly ran the comb through his thinning hair.

"Earl! Are you listening to me? What are you doing in there? If you want any of this, you'd better come on. I'm about ready to go to sleep."

"Go ahead, you old bag," Earl muttered under his breath. "You dole it out like it was gold anyhow. And I can testify that it ain't gold." He chuckled quietly.

Then for a few seconds, he closed his eyes and gave in to the need that never really left him. It was almost to fever pitch, but that was okay.

Tomorrow he could begin his quest to quench it.

ARCHER SAW the scrap of paper as soon as he turned into his driveway after following Resa to her apartment gates. It was fluttering precariously at the edge of his mailbox.

He slowed to a stop, eyeing the road and the surrounding area. *Nothing.*

He'd followed Resa home every night for a week. Tonight, Tuesday night, he'd anticipated seeing the dark sedan she'd noticed the two previous Tuesdays, but it hadn't showed.

If Resa was right, and he only followed her on Tuesdays, he must have seen Archer and aborted.

"So you left a note instead," Archer muttered. "Coward."

He pulled a small, high-powered flashlight out of his glove compartment and shone it on the scrap of paper. It was caught at the edge of the mailbox door, and he could see writing on it.

He wrinkled his brow. He didn't have an exam glove—not even a handkerchief. He'd have to grab the paper with his bare fingers and take a chance of contaminating it.

He glanced around the interior of his car for anything that would preserve the fingerprints and possible trace evidence on the note. On the floor on the passenger side, he spotted an empty envelope. He'd tossed it there the other day while glancing through his mail before he got out of his car.

Carefully, he used the tips of his thumb and index finger to grasp the edge of the note while he loosened the closure of the mailbox enough to slide it out. The breeze picked up just as the note came free and he almost lost it, but his damaged fingers managed to hold on.

With the note and his arms back inside his car window, he dropped the note into the envelope, and stuck the envelope in his inside coat pocket. He could barely resist pulling it out and reading it, but his detective's caution told him to wait until he was safely inside his house, with good lighting and a place to set the note so he wouldn't have to handle it.

It burned a hole in his jacket as he drove the fifty yards up the driveway to his Victorian house. He parked in the circular drive.

Just as he was getting out of his car, his cell phone rang. He looked at the caller ID and his heart slammed into his chest wall. It was Resa.

"Resa? What is it?"

"Archer?" Her voice was small and trembly. "You told me to call you first."

"What's the matter? Are you okay?"

"I don't know. There's—a note."

"Where? In your apartment?" Archer's heart rate tripled.

"Get out of there, Resa. Now!"

"It's not in my apartment—not exactly—" Her voice caught. He heard her take a shaky breath. "It's inside my windowsill. I think it was slipped underneath from the outside."

"Resa, listen to me. Have you checked your apartment?"

"Yes. Nothing's out of place. I don't think anybody's been inside."

"Good. Leave the note where it is. Call 911, and stay there with all the doors locked. Don't open the door to anyone until the police get there. I'm on my way."

"Archer? Hurry."

"Stay put, Resa."

He pocketed his phone, patted his jacket pocket to assure himself that the envelope was still there, and climbed back into his car.

On the way he called Clint and told him what Resa had told him. Clint said he'd meet the 911 team there.

Twenty-one long minutes later, Archer pulled up to the entrance to Resa's apartment complex. A uniformed officer he didn't know was stationed at the gate. Archer flashed his ID and explained that he was working on the Lock Rapist case as an independent investigator with Detective Banes.

The officer nodded. Clint had cleared him. He waved him through.

Ahead of him, Archer saw several parked police vehicles. He pulled up behind one and scanned the breezeways of the nearest apartment building. On the second floor, the front apartment's lights blazed, spotlighting an officer standing at the door.

He sprinted up the stairs. When he entered the apartment, he saw Resa sitting in a dining-room chair, her arms wrapped around herself, her eyes wide, her face pale. She saw him and her shoulders relaxed visibly.

Across the room, Clint glanced up from examining the inside of the windowsill. He gave Archer a slight nod, glanced at Resa, then went back to his job.

A kid who looked like a college student except for the badge pinned to his belt was balanced precariously on a tiny, non-functional fake balcony under the window and dusting the outside sill.

Archer reined in the urge to yell at the kid to watch where he parked his butt. This wasn't his case, he reminded himself. It was his ex-partner's.

Instead, he went over and knelt down beside Resa's chair. She reached out to him, her green eyes searching his face. After an instant's hesitation, he took her hand.

"I'm not sure they can decide if he was inside or not. Detective Banes said he could have slipped the note under the windowsill from the inside." Her voice quavered. "He thinks the Lock Rapist has been inside."

She squeezed his fingers and it took a lot of willpower not to wince.

"You did the right thing—almost. You got the phone calls backward." He gave her a little smile. "You should have called 911 first, then called me."

She nodded miserably. "You were the first person I thought of."

That surprised him. He frowned. The idea that she'd thought of him first scared him. Being someone's first choice in a crisis was the last thing he wanted. All he wanted was to be left alone.

The envelope in his jacket pocket burned his skin through the layers of fabric—a painful reminder that being left alone was no longer a choice. He was involved.

"Hey, you did good."

She pulled her hand free of his. Her fingers intertwined in her lap. Their knuckles turned white. He had an unwanted urge to touch her again. To untangle her fingers and rub them until warmth spread through them and up to put color back into her face.

He glanced at Clint, who was still involved in the evidence gathering.

"Resa," he said quietly. "Did you touch the note?"

"No," she said. "You told me not to."

"Could you read it?"

She nodded, pressing her lips together tightly.

"Tell me what it said."

She shut her eyes. Tears squeezed out between her closed lids. "It said, 'You can't shut me out. I'll get you.'"

He stood and patted her shoulder. "I'll be right back."

He stepped through the front door onto the concrete balustrade that connected the apartments.

"Hey, bud," he said to the young officer at the door. "Got a glove on you?"

"Sure, Detective." The officer dug in his pocket and pulled out a latex-free exam glove.

Archer took it and stretched it over his hand, then he retrieved the envelope from his pocket and slid the scrap of paper out of it.

Detective Archer. You're not as smart as you think you are. I'm looking forward to Theresa Wade. Think she'll be as good as her sister was? Or your wife? I'm pleased to be working with you again. If you release these two notes to the media, I might give you a break.

"Son of a—"

"Geoff." Clint appeared at his side. "What's that?"

He put the note inside the envelope and handed it to his ex-partner. "Resa's not the only one who got a note tonight."

Clint pulled the envelope open and peeked inside. "I'll be damned," he muttered. "It *is* the Lock Rapist."

"That's right. Now do you think you can put a guard on her?"

Clint sent Archer a frustrated look. "Don't you think I wish I could? I don't want any more attacks. But we're past stretched to the max. The president is on his way down here tomorrow to present some award to the Tennessee Valley Authority, so almost all my men are working double duty."

"She's in danger, Clint."

His ex-partner's green eyes darkened. "I understand that. I'm hoping I can free up an officer within a couple of days."

"A couple of days? What's she supposed to do in the meantime?"

"Come on, Geoff. What do you want me to do? I can't pull a babysitter out of thin air."

Archer felt frustration rise up in him like bile. "Damn it, Clint."

"You're so worried, why don't you keep her?"

"Me?" He laughed harshly.

"Sure. Let her stay with you until I can free somebody up."

"No. No way."

"Okay, then yeah, I guess she will be on her own."

He glared at Clint. "That's unacceptable. Okay.

Hell, why not? I'll take her home with me. She's already there till all hours of the night anyhow."

"Are you kidding me? You're not really considering it. You can barely take care of yourself."

"What does that mean? I'm doing just fine." He flexed his hand, stretching the shortened tendons and setting his jaw to keep from wincing. "If you're worried about my ability to protect her—if I have to shoot anybody, I'll just use a blowgun and poisoned darts."

Clint stared narrowly at him for a few seconds, his brows wrinkled with doubt. "I'll free up an officer as soon as I can." He looked down at his shoes, then back up. "Geoff, take care that she doesn't become a pawn in your self-destructive game. She's had a hard time."

Archer stared at him, anger burning through his nerve endings. "My self-destructive game? What the hell, Clint? Is that what you think I'm doing?"

Clint shrugged without speaking.

He clenched his fists. "Trust me, *Detective,*" he growled, "I have no intention of committing Suicide by Perp. If it comes down to him or me—it's going to be *him* on that cold slab in the morgue."

"So now you're a vigilante."

"Get off my case. You're the one who wanted me to protect her. You work on freeing up an officer to guard her. Meanwhile, she's going back with me."

"Well she's got to come downtown first, and give us a statement."

"Fine."

"Good."

Archer's scalp burned with the fury he was struggling to hold in check. Clint had no right acting so high and mighty. The Lock Rapist case had been his before it was Clint's. He was the one who'd failed to stop him, whose arrogance and certainty that he was doing the right thing had caused the rapist to escalate, and that had caused the death of his wife.

Keeping Resa Wade safe was his responsibility, because it was his fault that she was in danger.

RESA WATCHED the two men go head to head. She knew that Archer and Detective Banes had been partners before Archer was injured.

The two of them were alarmingly alike, and noticeably different. Both had dark hair and eyes. Both were tall—Archer was six feet, and Banes was a couple of inches taller than him. And both of them were obviously serious about their work.

Banes's face was more rounded. His stance was more relaxed, his demeanor friendlier.

Archer, on the other hand, was broodingly intense, his glances probing, his body spring-loaded, ready for anything. If he and Banes played good cop, bad cop, then Archer would definitely be the bad cop.

Oddly though, she'd much rather be under Archer's protection. Even though he was gruff and decidedly unfriendly, not to mention handicapped by his injured hand, he was the one she'd trust with her life.

The two men turned as one to look at her. Banes looked as if he'd lost a battle. Archer looked angry.

She felt like a bug under a microscope for the few seconds they stared at her. Then Archer stalked over to her side. "Pack a bag. You're going home with me."

"What?" She raised her eyebrows and uttered a short laugh. "No, I'm not."

He put a hand on the back of her chair and leaned over. "Don't make a scene. You're going to end up going with me anyway."

"I don't understand."

"Nashville P.D. doesn't have enough manpower to place you into protective custody."

"Protective custody?"

He nodded. "Until the police can free up someone to guard you in a safe house you're coming with me."

His authoritative tone that she'd just five minutes ago thought was reassuring now raised her hackles. "And I don't have any say-so in this?"

He met her gaze and his dark eyes glimmered with something she might think was amusement, if it were anyone but Archer. "Nope."

He straightened, but she caught his arm. "Does Detective Banes know you're doing this?"

When he nodded, a splinter of fear stabbed her. "Why? What's happened? I know you don't want me around."

"Come on. It's after midnight, and you've still got to sign your statement." He took a step back, enough to remove her hand from his arm.

Resa stood. Apprehension masked the weariness

that had weighed her down earlier. Something had happened. Something significant. More certain than the vague note she'd received.

She'd known Archer only a week, but that was long enough to know how much he valued his privacy. How desperately he wanted to bury himself in that basement firing range of his and never come out.

There was only one reason he'd give all that up. Only one reason he'd even consider taking on the responsibility for keeping her safe.

He thought he had the chance to catch the man who'd destroyed his life.

"It is the Lock Rapist, isn't it?" She caught his arm again. "You've confirmed it."

He looked down at her fingers, then raised his gaze to hers. "Yes. You're not the only one who got a note."

"What do you mean?"

"There was a note in my mailbox when I got back from following you home."

"You got a note, too?"

Archer nodded.

"Well, what did it say?"

His gaze faltered. "Basically, just that he wants me to release these notes to the media."

"Good. That's easy enough."

Archer didn't look up. His fingers worried a corner of the note.

"Archer?" she said. "There's something more, isn't there? What is it? What else does he say in your note?"

Archer folded the note, but before he could cram

it into his pocket, Resa caught his arm. "I want to know what it says. I have a right to know."

He flipped the piece of paper open and handed it to her. She read it out loud.

"'Detective Archer. You're not as smart as you think you are. I'm looking forward to Theresa Wade. Think she'll be as good as her sister was? Or your wife? I'm pleased to be working with you again. If you release these two notes to the media, I might give you a break.' Looking forward to—me." Her fingers went to her mouth. "He *is* after me. Because he thinks I can identify him?"

"And I think he's using you to get to me."

"And you're planning to use me as bait to catch him."

Chapter Four

Archer stared at Resa as her words rang in his ears. Was that what he was doing? Using her to exact his revenge? He didn't think so. But hearing her say it— thrown at him as an accusation—he felt a tiny, niggling doubt creep in. He thrust it aside.

"No," he said evenly. "I would never place another person's life in jeopardy just to get revenge."

She pinned him with those dark-green eyes. "Maybe not *just,* but if it happened to be a side effect, can you honestly say you'd decline the opportunity?"

"Now you're arguing semantics. Would I go after the Lock Rapist if I had the chance? Absolutely. Is that my sole reason for wanting to protect you? Absolutely not."

Resa made a face. "I hate it when people ask questions and answer them themselves."

Archer gave her a wry smile. "Okay, truce. I'll stop asking and answering annoying questions if you'll stop painting me as a bloodthirsty vigilante."

Her mouth turned up in a sheepish grin. "Fine. You've got a deal."

"Now, are we straight? You're going home with me until Clint has the staff to set you up in a safe house?"

Resa took a step toward him, pushing her way past the boundary of his personal space. "On one condition. You teach me to shoot."

He arched an eyebrow at her. "Seriously? You still plan to keep that gun?"

"I do, and I'd be a poor gun owner if I didn't learn everything about my weapon, wouldn't I?"

She was determined. He'd seen that from the beginning. And now, after hearing her admit that he was the first person she'd thought of when she was in fear for her life, he had no choice.

He was bound to protect her.

"Ms. Wade?" Clint stepped up behind her and touched her elbow.

She turned her head toward the detective but didn't break eye contact with Archer.

"You'll need to come to the station to make a statement."

"Of course." She turned to look at Clint. "What's the address?"

Archer slid his hand along the small of her back. "Clint, can't she do the statement in the morning? She's nearly asleep on her feet."

His friend eyed him narrowly. Archer could practically hear his thoughts. *Is there something going on*

*between Archer and Resa? Just what kind of instruct-
ing is he doing inside his sprawling Victorian house?*

He flattened his lips and sent Clint a disgusted
look. "Nothing's going to change between now and
tomorrow morning."

Clint gave an elaborate shrug. "Get her there by nine."

"Will do." He turned to Resa, but Clint stopped him
with a hand on his arm.

"Geoff, I need to talk to you a minute."

Resa nodded as Archer followed Clint across the
room. "What's the big secret, Clint? I thought we
were done here."

"Geoff, I'm not sure it's a good idea for you to take
Resa with you."

"Why not? You've already made it clear you can't
spare anyone to protect her."

"I'm just concerned about your—"

"My what? My mental state? My ability to protect
her? We've been over that already."

"No. You're obviously still blaming yourself for everything that's happened. You've got to get over it.
Cutting off the media circus surrounding the Lock
Rapist was the right thing to do. It should have forced
him into the open, trying to garner more attention."

"Yeah. Well, it did." Bitterness scratched his throat.
He'd forced him into the open, all right. The monster
had veered from his pattern and gone after Natalie.

A crime scene investigator approached. "We're
done, Detective."

"Good. Thanks." Clint looked around the room.

"Okay, everybody. We're done here. Gather up your stuff and let's get back to the station. I want evidence reports and theories first thing in the morning." He spoke to Archer again. "I'll see you and Resa in the morning."

Archer gave him a curt nod. "I want to hear about the fingerprint evidence, and anything else they find here. Don't shut me out of the investigation again, Clint. I need all the information I can get to protect her."

Resa stood near the front door waiting for Archer to finish talking with Clint. Despite her half-hearted efforts not to eavesdrop, she'd heard nearly every word Archer had said, and most of what Detective Banes said.

So now she knew why Archer had agreed to take her home with him. He felt he'd screwed up the investigation by cutting off the media attention surrounding the Lock Rapist. He thought his wife's death was his fault, and so were the two attacks since then—including her sister's.

So she had her choice of what to believe—revenge or guilt. Whatever his reason, Geoffrey Archer was going to dog her footsteps until the Lock Rapist was caught or until Detective Banes could provide police protection for her.

Archer's hand touched the small of her back again—warm and reassuring. "Ready to go? My car's right out front."

"Oh, no," she countered, raising a hand to stop him right there. "I'm not going to be stuck out there with no means of transportation. I'll take my own car."

His hand slid around her waist from the back and his head bent until his mouth was near her ear. "Do you understand that your life may be in danger?"

His preemptive tone irritated her. "I understand that perfectly. What *you* don't seem to understand is that I've taken care of myself all my life, as well as raising my sister, and I see no reason to change now. Despite what you and Detective Banes think, I am capable of being cautious. But I can tell you right now there's no way I'm going to be stuck miles from town with no car. I have a job. I can't afford to take time off. If I don't finish and deliver the outfits on time, not only will I lose those clients, I'll be branded as unreliable. And the music business is a small town. I'd never sell another design."

He looked down his nose at her. "I could have sworn you told me you understood how serious this is."

"I do understand. And the idea that someone wants to hurt me is terrifying. But I can't put my life on hold—"

He held up both hands in a gesture of surrender. "Let's ignore for the moment that protective custody is the very *definition* of putting your life on hold— long enough to avoid being killed. Look, just drop it. It's way too late to argue about it tonight. Take your car. We'll sort out where you will and won't go tomorrow."

Resa took a long cleansing breath and felt the tightness in her neck and shoulders relax minutely. She knew she hadn't won, but at least he'd called a truce for tonight.

"Thank you. Now will you help me load my sewing machine and supplies into my car?"

Judging by his scowl, he already regretted taking on the responsibility of guarding her.

EARLY THE NEXT morning Archer sat in his desk chair with his forearms resting on his knees. His right hand gripped a spring-resistance hand and finger exerciser. It was configured like trumpet keys. He squeezed, concentrating on pressing with equal pressure on all four finger keys. Of course, his fingers didn't cooperate.

He clenched his teeth, staring at his index finger as if he could force it to work right by sheer will. The tendons that had been shredded by the bullet were shortened. Straightening all four fingers was almost impossible, and placing any significant strain on his index finger sent pain surging through it. Pain that radiated up his thumb and wrist, caused by the tiny nerve endings that had been torn.

He squeezed harder. His hand cramped. The exercise grip clattered to the floor. He blurted out a curse and stood and kicked it across the room. It slammed against the opposite wall.

Then he remembered he wasn't alone. Resa was upstairs.

He glanced through his office door at the stairs that led to the first floor. He'd closed the door at the top, which cut off most noise from the basement.

Still, knowing she was under his roof made him feel exposed and vulnerable. He rubbed his freshly shaven cheeks and chin. What the hell had he been thinking, bringing her here?

He couldn't protect anyone. Hell, he could barely function. For the past fifteen months he'd existed on little more than coffee and guilt. He'd had only one goal, one reason to look forward to each day. The possibility that he could one day confront the Lock Rapist and force him to look down the barrel of the gun that would kill him.

But now, out of some misguided notion of making up for not stopping the rapist, he'd taken on the responsibility for the welfare of another human being. He'd promised Resa Wade things he couldn't deliver—safety and protection.

He flexed the fingers of his right hand, watching the white scars stretch and pull. Then he held up his left hand—strong and whole. He still had an hour or so until he had to wake Resa.

The least he could do was continue to train his left hand to take over for his ruined right one. He opened the top left drawer of his desk and took out his SIG 9mm and a box of cartridges. Then he walked over to the firing lane he used for his practice sessions.

Grimly, he ejected the magazine and loaded it. Then he slapped it back into place.

Wrapping his left hand around the grip, he raised the gun one-handed and fired—again and again and again.

WHEN RESA opened her eyes, for an instant she didn't know where she was. The light fell across her bed in the wrong direction. The bed itself felt different.

She lay still for a moment. Something else was different, too. Something inside her. The fear and guilt that had weighted her down ever since her sister's attack had lessened. And the reason took the shape of strong broad shoulders and piercing eyes.

Archer. She sat up and looked around. She was in Archer's house. In his bed—well, one of his beds. His car had ridden her tail all the way out to his house; he'd grabbed her sewing supplies and dressmaker's form out of her trunk and deposited them in this second-floor bedroom in record time. Then he'd pointed out the adjoining bath, told her the bed linens were clean, promised to wake her at eight, and disappeared.

She chuckled under her breath. It was almost comical, how determined he'd been to get away from her. She pushed back the covers and got up. Glancing at her watch, she was surprised to see that it was barely after seven. Six hours' sleep, and she felt refreshed. She yawned and stretched. She couldn't remember the last time she'd actually started the morning feeling rested.

She was glad for the extra hour to get ready. After a leisurely shower, she pulled her hair back in a ponytail and dressed in a body-skimming linen dress and sandals. A little eye makeup and a dab of foundation and she was ready to go.

Looking at her sewing machine, she calculated the amount of time she needed to finish the outfits for the awards ceremony. As she'd expected, time was going to be tight.

With a last glance in the mirror over the old dresser, she stepped out into the hall. There was one other bedroom on this floor—Archer's room. As she headed for the stairs, she glanced in through its open door. There were no lights on and the draperies were closed.

A shirt was draped over a desk chair. The bedcovers had been hastily smoothed, and the bathroom door was ajar. He was up—it looked as if he'd been up for hours.

She descended the stairs and went looking for the kitchen. It was at the back of the house, through the living room and dining room.

Archer wasn't there. Resa glanced at the empty coffeepot, debating whether she should make coffee. Quickly deciding that he might resent her feeling that much at home, she circled through a laundry room and out into a wide hall that led back to the foyer.

This area she knew. She'd come in through the heavy hardwood front door every evening for the past two weeks. Next to the polished wood staircase that led to the second floor was the door to the firing range.

She pushed it open. The stairwell was dark, but a weak light shone beyond the foot of the stairs. Archer was probably downstairs in his office.

She considered turning around and going back to the kitchen, or even sneaking upstairs and pretending to have just finished dressing. She wasn't ready to confront him—not on his own turf. She decided to go back up to the kitchen and wait for him.

As she stepped backward to close the door, she heard a muffled crack—the distinctive sound of a handgun being fired in a cubicle. Then she heard the gun hit the concrete floor.

She hurried down the stairs. Archer's office was empty. She walked down the long bank of lanes in the direction from which the sounds had come.

As she approached lane ten, she saw his shadow. He was bending down to retrieve something. The shadow straightened, and she heard a litany of colorful and inventive curses.

She stepped around the corner of the cubicle in time to see him place a large 9mm gun in his right hand, much as he'd done for her the other night. He supported his right hand with his left, and held it aimed at the target.

But something was wrong. The more tightly he gripped the gun's barrel, the more his hand shook. But still he tried. He stretched his fingers, then gripped the handle again.

His hand jerked, and the gun slipped. He caught it in his left hand before it hit the counter. A quiet groan escaped his lips.

Resa gasped. She'd had no idea how bad the injury to his hand was.

Archer froze.

She waited for him to turn around, pin her with his dark stare, and make some biting comment about her sneaking up on him.

But he didn't move. His back was stiff and tight. She could hear his rapid breathing.

She couldn't take her eyes off him. His hair that just missed brushing his collar and the sharp, tense line of his jaw made his neck look vulnerable.

She wanted to smooth a tendril that had waved the wrong way. As soon as she acknowledged her desire, it morphed into an obsession. Her hand rose.

"Get out of here."

His voice was a growl so low, so controlled, that she barely heard it, and yet its tone chilled her.

"Archer, I'm sorry, I—"

"Get out," he snapped without turning around.

She backed away and turned and ran up the stairs, not stopping until she got to the kitchen. For a few seconds she stood there in the dark, hugging herself.

How did he do it? How did anyone exercise that much control over his emotions? She knew his wife's death had been horrifying and devastating. She'd seen newspaper and TV accounts of how he'd walked in on her just as she was raising the gun to her temple. When he'd tried to stop her she'd turned the gun on him.

He'd caught a bullet in his right hand, and his wife had killed herself.

Resa closed her eyes and shook her head as waves of anguish squeezed her heart. He had experienced what she feared would happen to her sister. Celia had been on the verge of suicide more than once since her attack. Resa already carried a huge burden of guilt and regret because Celia was attacked while she was living with her. She couldn't imagine how she would go on if Celia committed suicide.

Not only had Archer had to live with his wife's suicide, he had to live with a damaged hand, a destroyed career and the knowledge that his wife had wanted to die so badly that she'd been willing to kill him rather than allow him to stop her. Wrenching grief tore through her at what he'd been through.

She put her hands to her cheeks and tried to stop the distressing thoughts.

A glance at the kitchen clock told her that they needed to leave soon if they were going to be at the police station by nine.

She ran cool water over her wrists and touched her temples with her wet fingers, working to compose herself. Then she forced herself to think about inane things, like making coffee.

She finally found the coffee grounds, coffee filters and mugs. It took her a few minutes, but by the time the coffee was made, she'd calmed down.

She'd poured herself a mug, sweetened it and sat down at the huge, scarred kitchen table when Archer appeared in the doorway.

She looked up, mildly surprised by his appearance. She'd never paid attention to his clothes, but now she did. He wore impeccably tailored dress pants and a hunter-green shirt with a patterned tie. With his broad shoulders, lean belly and long, strong legs, he could have been a *GQ* model.

His face, though, shocked her. She'd expected him to be furious, or coldly silent after she'd witnessed his failure with his gun. But he looked haggard, as if he hadn't slept a wink. His hair was damp from the shower, and he'd shaved, but the razor hadn't removed the lines around his mouth or the faint blue circles under his eyes.

"Are you all right?" she asked.

He nodded shortly. "Ready?"

"Sure." She set down her mug. "Where's the station?"

He told her.

"Good. I'll take my car. I need to run some errands—"

Archer gave her a look that closed her throat.

They would not go in two cars today.

EARL FLOPPED down on the crisply made bed and stretched out, the heels of his shoes scraping across the bedspread. He chuckled. His wife and kids would be gone for at least a week, maybe longer.

He'd told his boss that he needed a week off for some minor surgery, so now he was totally free. He had plenty of time to plan and execute a perfect attack.

He'd already picked out his victim. He'd had his eye on the waifish blonde for weeks, ever since he'd installed a home security system for her. It hadn't taken him five minutes to figure out that she was a single mother. No husband. No boyfriend. Just her and her little boy.

She was practically perfect. He wasn't happy that there was a child involved, but he'd already become obsessed with her blond hair and delicate bone structure. So much like his mother's.

He'd already checked out the neighborhood, too. Now, all he needed to do was choose a night and a time. Then he could be done. The urge would go away. For a while.

He settled back for a daydream of how he'd sneak in quietly so as not to wake her little boy. How he'd cover her face and overpower her. Then when he was done, how he'd gently and reverently cut a lock of her pale hair.

But suddenly the hair was dark, and her face morphed into Theresa Wade's.

The excitement he'd felt as he'd planted the notes for her and Archer washed over him. He closed his eyes and gave in to the rush of adrenaline that surged like blood through his whole body, engorging him.

He imagined overpowering Theresa. Her type didn't appeal to him. She wasn't blond, wasn't fragile and vulnerable like her sister, like his carefully chosen victims. Like his mother had been.

Yet for some reason he felt compelled to take her— and not just because she thought she could stop him. He had another more satisfying reason. Through her he could torment Archer.

His attack on Archer's wife had done more than he'd hoped. It had destroyed Archer's career and given Earl the satisfaction of a double revenge. It was pure luck and a bonus for him that Natalie Archer had been just his type.

But although Archer had quit the force after his wife's death, the new lead detective kept the media blackout in place.

And that really ticked off Earl. He needed the news coverage. The speculation, the endless interviews with victims and families and neighbors, with psychologists, police, all talking about *him.*

"See, Mom?" he whispered. "You always said I could be famous. Always said you'd be so proud of me. You're proud of me now, aren't you?"

His mom had watched TV constantly. She'd sung along with the commercials and gotten him to sing, too.

"You work hard, Earl baby," she said, "and you can be on TV someday. Wouldn't that be wonderful? Then Mommy can watch you all day long."

He knew she was watching. He could feel her approval. Why, they'd even given him a name—the Lock Rapist, because of the lock of hair he took. It was funny as hell that the name they'd given him had a double meaning. He was an expert at installing security systems. There wasn't a lock out there that he couldn't get past.

He pulled the slip of paper with the young mother's address on it out of his shirt pocket and closed his eyes. But he couldn't remember what she looked like. All he could think of was Theresa.

He wadded up the paper in his fist. The little blonde

would have to wait. He couldn't concentrate on anything else until he'd taken care of Theresa Wade and Detective Archer.

Chapter Five

"Are you always this pleasant?" Resa asked Archer when he showed up in the kitchen a couple of mornings after their silent trip to and from the police station. She finished filling a mug with coffee and held it out. "Or are you making a special effort because you have company?"

He frowned at her as he grabbed the mug. She filled another one for herself and set the carafe back on the coffeemaker.

When she turned, he was seated at the scarred kitchen table, staring into his coffee. If possible, he looked worse than he had the first morning. She sat down across from him and sipped her coffee while she tried to contain her growing irritation. Being sad or guilt-ridden or in pain was one thing. But this protracted foul mood was more than she could take.

She wanted to yell at him. Throw her coffee on him. Anything to force him to act like a normal human being. She'd liked him better when he was gruffly showing her how to hold the gun.

She took a deep breath. "I think I'm going to pack up my stuff today and head back to my apartment."

That roused him. His dark gaze slammed into hers. "The hell you are."

She lifted her shoulders in a tiny shrug.

He doubled his fist and banged it on the table. It would have been more effective if it hadn't so obviously hurt him.

She resisted the urge to cover his hand with hers to try to ease the pain.

"Where'd you get such a harebrained idea? Doesn't it mean anything to you that he knows where you live?"

"Of course it worries me that he knows where I live. But, you've made it *painfully* obvious that you don't want me here."

He wrapped the fingers of his left hand around his mug and took a long swig of coffee. Then he went back to staring into it. "I want you to be safe."

"But you wish I wasn't here."

He didn't deny it. After a beat he said, "You're— distracting."

Resa's pulse jumped. *Distracting.* Had he really said that? She'd already decided that *he* was distracting. That was one reason she wanted to get out of his house. As big as it was, it wasn't big enough.

Her fascination with him floated like a ghost through the walls and floors of the sprawling Victorian, tormenting her. She'd discovered that she could tell where he was at any time, through some combination of attraction and intuition and sixth sense. She didn't like that.

"Distracting how? And what are you trying to do that you can't, because of my beguiling presence?"

A tiny movement of his mouth made her think he was struggling not to smile. "I'm studying all the case files on the Lock Rapist. I keep thinking there's something I've missed. There's no such thing as a perfect crime. He has to have slipped up somewhere."

She sat down and wrapped her hands around her mug. "Let me see them. I want to understand him the way you and Detective Banes do. I want to know what you see in his profile, what his patterns are, how—" She paused for an instant. "How he picks his victims."

"No."

"Why not? I could help."

"Why would you want to know all that? He attacked your sister. Why does the reason matter to you?"

"What if it was me he was after? It was my apartment."

"You're not his type."

"His type? He has a *type?* See, this is what I'm talking about. What is his type? How does he pick his victims?"

Archer sent her an exasperated look. "The media gave him the name the Lock Rapist because he cuts a lock of hair from each victim and leaves another lock at the scene."

"The hair he left beside Celia was from his previous victim. That's gruesome." She paused. "Celia didn't say anything about him cutting her hair."

"She apparently doesn't remember him doing it. And the fact that he takes a piece of his victim's hair wasn't released to the press."

Resa took a sip of her coffee. "What else wasn't released to the press—or to me?"

"A couple of things. Nothing you need to know."

"You don't want to tell me."

Once again, he didn't speak.

"Nice to know you trust me," she said wryly. "What do you think the lock of hair means?"

"Nobody but him knows that. The most likely guess is that it has to do with whatever trauma in his past led him to rape."

"Do you have a theory?"

Archer shook his head. "Nope. It's not a good idea to start fantasizing about the perp's trigger event. There are things you can generalize, but it's almost impossible to predict what exactly happened to cause this guy to turn to rape while another with an similar background ends up as—say, a social worker or victims' advocate."

"What are the usual reasons?"

"I'm sure you've watched the true crime stories. Everything from sexual or physical abuse at a young age to witnessing a traumatic event. And some people are just evil."

"Really? You believe that?"

"Don't you? Look what this monster did to your sister. Would you rather think he couldn't help it because his mother beat him?"

"Well, whatever happened to him, how can he brutally attack six women and not leave any evidence?"

"That's the sixty-four-thousand-dollar question." Archer ran a hand over his face, then rubbed his eyes. They were red, and blue smudges underlined them.

"You're exhausted." She glanced at her watch. "I have two appointments for fittings out in West Meade. Ten o'clock and eleven-thirty. Why don't you take a nap while I'm gone? I can wake you when I get back, or you can just sleep as long as you want to."

He shook his head.

"I promise I'll go straight there and come straight back here. It's about a forty-five-minute drive. Unless my clients have decided to ruin my life by rejecting my designs, I should be done by two o'clock."

"I have class. Two classes, actually. Forensics and crime scene investigation. I'm giving the students a prep day before the final exam. I'll be on my cell phone." Archer stood and picked up his mug. He set it in the sink, then put his hand on the back of her chair.

"Don't stop anywhere else," he said, his breath tickling her cheek and sending a shiver through her. "Not even for gas. If you see anything odd—even if you just get a feeling—call me. I'll have a uniform on your tail within seconds."

She pushed herself out of the chair and away from him. "No problem, boss. I'll be a good girl."

His eyes snapped. "This isn't a joke."

"I know." She swallowed. At a distance, Archer

was disconcerting. Up close he could steal her breath and muddle her thoughts with one word, one subtle movement.

"I'd better get going." She escaped upstairs, lecturing herself each step of the way. What was the matter with her?

Archer was the worst possible man for her to be attracted to. He was grieving, he was in pain and he obviously didn't want to be around anybody, certainly not her.

You're distracting. As she gathered up her supplies and put them in her carrying case, she pondered what he meant by that. Was he just complaining about having someone around to interrupt his reclusive lifestyle? Or was she distracting because she was a woman? A tiny thrill swirled through her chest.

"And that would be a good thing how?" she berated herself. She was barely holding it together herself. The last thing she needed was an emotional entanglement with a surly grouch like him.

Besides, as far as she could tell, he hadn't even noticed that she was a woman.

FOUR HOURS LATER, Resa finally finished with her last scheduled fitting. The first two had taken about fifteen minutes each. But this client, Chastity Sloan, one of the new, brash young country stars, was a whole different story. Chastity loved Resa's design of a low-slung suede skirt with a silver-buckled belt and silver-accented cowboy boots. She also loved the midriff-baring turquoise top with silver and turquoise beads sewn into the low neckline.

But she wanted the skirt lower and the midriff of the top higher. Resa tried to tell her she wouldn't be able to walk, much less gyrate around the stage, if the skirt were cut any lower, but Chastity, twenty and already a diva, insisted.

As Resa walked out to her car, she played over in her mind the things she should have said.

"I am such a wimp," she whispered. She should have refused on creative grounds. It was *her* design, after all. But she'd never been paid so much for a single outfit, and she needed the money in case Celia had to be hospitalized. In the end, money won out over creativity and personal integrity.

She lifted her hair off her hot neck and muttered a fairly explicit curse as she walked down the long brick walkway.

"That's right," she scolded herself. "Go slinking off to hide in Archer's house. I hope the money was worth it." She glanced around to make sure nobody was close enough to hear her. She almost never talked to herself.

The street, which boasted houses that sold in the millions of dollars, was quiet. The only sounds were a lawn edger two houses down, and the fading rumble of a car engine at the far end of the street. Glancing that way, she saw the rear fender of a dark car as it turned onto a cross street.

Just as she pressed the remote to unlock her car, her

cell phone rang. She groped around in her purse and finally found it. It was Archer.

"Where are you?" he growled.

"I'm just fine. How are you?"

He was silent.

Irritation streaked through her, tightening her scalp. There was a limit to how much self-pitying garbage she could deal with from him. She was packing up and getting out of there today. "I'm just now leaving my second appointment. We had a couple of *creative* disagreements. She won."

"Come straight home."

She bit back a retort and rolled her eyes. "Yes, sir."

He disconnected.

"Damn, Archer. Are you trying to be the biggest ass on the block?"

She reached out to open the driver's side rear door just as his words registered.

Come straight home. Her pulse jumped. Had he really said *home?* Even if he had, it didn't mean anything. It was an expression, that was all. She shrugged off the feeling of warmth and safety that enveloped her because he was concerned about her.

She threw her bags onto the backseat, slammed the door, and opened the driver's-side door.

She froze, her hand on the hot door handle.

There was a piece of paper in the middle of the driver's seat. She frowned at it. It couldn't be hers. It was yellow lined paper, and she never used that.

Unease crawled like a spider up her spine as she

glanced up and down the street. *Nothing.* Even the edger she'd noticed a couple of minutes before had stopped.

The car. She looked back toward the far end of the street where the car had turned, and any sense of safety dissolved like an ice cube in hot water. The car had been dark—black or dark blue.

Was it him? Her eyes went back to the note. The paper was from a generic note pad that could have been bought anywhere. She wondered if he'd written the note with a generic number-2 pencil that could have been bought anywhere.

Her chest ached and, belatedly, she realized she wasn't breathing. She gasped, her lungs craving air. Her right hand was fisted against her midsection, and her left hand was hot—she was still holding on to the door handle. She shivered, despite the summer sun.

Everything seemed magnified—louder, brighter. Her scalp tingled. Her pulse pounded in her ears and fluttered in her throat. She felt faint.

She surveyed the houses and cars on the street. Maybe it was someone handing out coupons for a pizza place, or some kid looking for a donation for his senior trip.

As soon as the thoughts surfaced, she knew how ridiculous they were. She gave her head a little shake, trying to think rationally. Trying to push past the paralyzing fear.

She licked her lips and worked on controlling her breathing. There was no innocuous explanation. *The note was on a torn piece of paper. And he'd put it inside her car.*

She glanced frantically up and down the street, then with shaking fingers she unlocked the car. She brushed the note off the floorboard, climbed in, started the engine and sped away.

She gripped the steering wheel with a death grip and vowed that nothing would stop her from getting home to Archer as soon as possible.

Then she had a horrible thought. What if *he* had tampered with her tires, or her steering? What if her car broke down and he was lying in wait to "rescue" her? She had no idea what he looked like. He could be anybody.

Stop it—stop it—*stop it.*

She turned on the radio. It was on a country station and the high-pitched twang of bluegrass filled her car, drowning out the sound of her thoughts.

She could do it. She could make it home—to Archer.

ARCHER LEANED OVER and sniffed at the skillet. Almost perfect. He crushed another clove of garlic and added it to the simmering mixture of butter, olive oil, fresh spinach, pine nuts and jumbo shrimp. He'd already cooked the pasta and opened a bottle of wine.

He wasn't sure why he was going to so much trouble to make nice with Resa. Although that wasn't the only reason he was cooking. He was hungry. He ignored the little voice that reminded him there was sliced ham and Swiss cheese in the refrigerator, and fresh rye bread in the bread box.

Okay, maybe he did feel a little bad about how mean he'd been ever since she got here. He knew he'd over-reacted the other morning down in the firing range when he'd realized she was standing behind him. But she'd surprised him and he'd felt furious and humiliated.

Nobody had seen how bad his hand was. Not even his fellow cops. The only one who knew was Banes. But now *she* knew. He'd seen the pity in her eyes when he'd come up to the kitchen later.

Pity. It had felt just the way he'd known it would. It cut like a razor, stung like sweat in the eyes, sickened like a punch to the gut.

But that wasn't the only reason he'd been in such a foul mood. She'd noticed this morning that he looked exhausted. He was.

When he'd told her she was distracting, he'd been telling the truth. He hadn't realized when he'd told Clint he'd take her home with him just how distracting she'd turn out to be. The idea that she was in bed across the hall from him had tormented him for three nights. He hadn't slept a wink, and not even cold showers helped.

He couldn't deny that she was a lovely, sexy woman. Nor could he convince himself that her sassy talk and determined bravery didn't pull at his rusty heartstrings.

He gave the pasta sauce a last stir, turned off the burner, and looked at his watch. Where was she? It had been over an hour since he'd called her. She should be home by now.

He stepped over to the kitchen counter, to where a bottle of sauvignon blanc sat breathing. He'd had a devil of a time getting it open. Good wine was a weakness of his, but just then he'd have given anything for a cheap, screw-cap bottle, although he'd have probably had trouble with that, too. His hand was getting stronger, but twisting and grasping tightly were still a problem.

He looked at his watch again. *Damn it.* If she didn't get here within the next five minutes, he was calling Clint to put out an APB on her car.

The door between the foyer and his living room opened. He listened. Heavy footsteps echoed across the hardwood floors. It was Frank.

The white-haired retired police sergeant appeared at the kitchen door. "Hey, Geoff, I'm ready to go. Need anything?"

He shook his head and held up the wine bottle. "Want some wine before you go?"

"Nah. I'm good. Linda promised me a steak for dinner."

Archer nodded. "How was it today?"

"Not bad. That group of college kids came this afternoon."

"Right. Who took care of showing them the various weapons?"

Frank named a lieutenant from the precinct near the school. "Anyhow, I'd better get home. See you Monday."

"Thanks, Frank."

A few minutes after Frank left, he heard the front door open. Relief washed over him. He had to stop himself from running into the foyer. Instead he took two wineglasses, set them on the table and poured the wine.

When he heard her heels on the hardwood floor, he looked up.

She stood in the doorway between the dining room and kitchen, looking small and thin. When his gaze met hers, a shard of fear ripped through him. Her eyes were wide and dark, and shining with pure terror.

"Resa, what is it?"

She lifted her hand and he saw the piece of yellow lined paper sitting on a tissue. Then she swayed and the paper fluttered to the floor.

He was beside her instantly, wrapping his arm around her and leading her to a chair.

She sat woodenly, her hands folded in her lap.

He pulled another chair up beside her and sat, then picked up a wineglass. "Here," he said softly. "Drink this."

She took the glass in both hands and sipped at it. After a few seconds she set the glass down, squeezed her eyes shut and rubbed her temples.

"Tell me what happened. Are you hurt?"

She opened her eyes and shook her head. Her face was ghostly pale, which made her eyes look enormous.

"No. Archer—the note."

He glanced down at the torn piece of yellow lined paper as fear and fury warred inside him. He grabbed an exam glove from a drawer and pulled it on, then went over and picked up the note. He set it on the table.

"What does it say?" he asked her.

She shook her head. "I don't know. I didn't read it."

He pulled it toward him. If she hadn't read it, he wanted to see it first, before he showed it to her.

Using the tines of a fork to hold it still, he unfolded it with his gloved hand and read it silently.

See, Theresa, I can get to you any time I want. Like right now. You're not my type but you're associating with my sworn enemy, and that makes you very interesting to me.

He cursed under his breath. "Where was this?"

"On my car seat."

"Did you leave your car unlocked?" He heard the hard edge to his voice but he couldn't hold back. He never should have let her go out alone. He should have known the bastard would try something.

She shook her head and sipped some more wine. A little color was beginning to return to her cheeks. "Of course not. He somehow got it unlocked." She took a shaky breath. "How could he do that on an empty street in a ritzy neighborhood like that?"

He didn't bother answering.

"What does it say?"

He turned the sheet of paper so she could read it. What little color she'd regained drained from her face.

"I don't understand. What does he want with me?"

"Just like he says, you're in his way. You're causing him a problem." He took the wineglass and set it down, then took her hand. Her fingers were icy. "He can't hurt you here, Resa. We'll get him."

She squeezed his hand and panic rushed up to clog his throat. What was he doing? He didn't want her depending on him.

He pulled away and stood, ignoring the voice inside him that said *You should have thought of that before you brought her here.*

"I've got to call Clint. He needs this note to analyze and compare with the others." He pulled his cell phone from his pocket and pressed the speed-dial button for Clint's cell phone.

Clint answered on the first ring.

"Clint. Resa received another note. This one was left inside her locked car."

"There on your property?"

"No. Over in West Meade. She was fitting an outfit she'd designed for a country music star."

"Why didn't she call us?"

"I haven't gotten that far with her yet."

"So she got into her car and drove back there? Hell, any trace evidence has probably been destroyed."

"Yeah, well." He glanced at her. She was watching him, her eyes still wide and dark in her pale face. "She came straight back here. Whatever evidence is left, I'd think you'd want to get it ASAP."

"I do. We'll be right over."

"Hey, Clint. Do me a favor will you? Come in unmarked cars. Don't do the sirens and blue lights."

"Okay. See you in a few."

He disconnected and turned to Resa. "How about some pasta for dinner?"

She shook her head. "I'm not hungry."

"Well, you've got to eat or that wine you drank will go to your head."

"Then bottoms up." Picking up the glass, she gestured toward him with it. "I think I'd like to see the world through a haze for a while."

He took the glass from her unsteady hand. "No, you wouldn't. Now sit down and let me serve you some pasta and French bread. I'll get you a glass of water."

Her eyes began to fill up with fear again.

"Hey." He gently turned her head back toward him. "If you're good, I'll let you have another glass of wine after you eat. Deal?"

She gave him a watery smile and nodded. "Deal."

BY THE TIME Detective Banes and his team were through processing her car for evidence, Resa was a nervous wreck. Archer's pasta was delicious, but she couldn't manage more than a couple of bites. And those stuck in her throat.

Then Banes came in to take her statement. He whispered something to Archer and Archer muttered a reply, glared at him and left.

"Can't he stay?" she asked.

Detective Banes gave her a reassuring smile. "He's

taking a look at what the crime scene unit found. Why don't you tell me what happened?"

He didn't want Archer interfering with her questioning. Resa described what had happened as succinctly as she could. She told him about the car she'd spotted, and the house three doors down where someone had been running a lawn edger. Otherwise the street had been deserted.

"So you got there around twelve-thirty?"

"Right. I looked at my dashboard clock."

"And you were in the house until three?"

She nodded. "When I finally got into the car, it was 3:05."

"And you never went outside? Didn't have to get something out of your car? Didn't look out a window?"

"No. We were doing the fittings in my client's bedroom suite on the back of the house."

"Did you leave your car door unlocked? Or your window cracked a little?"

"No."

"Be sure, Ms. Wade. It was hot. Maybe you lowered the window just enough to let some air in while you were inside."

Resa raised her chin slightly. "I didn't."

"Okay. I've got someone searching the newspaper archives, but back in December when your sister was attacked, was your picture ever in the paper? Any newspaper in any town?"

"Not that I know of. Why?"

"I'm just trying to get a feel for how the Lock

Rapist found you." Detective Banes rubbed his chin and studied her. "Have you been here in Nashville ever since your sister's attack?"

"Yes. I mean—I've spent a lot of time at my mother's, helping her to take care of my sister."

"Your sister isn't doing well?"

Resa shook her head. "She had a breakdown after the attack. She's not eating, not sleeping. Hardly communicates at all."

"I'm sorry. So how much time would you say you've spent at your mother's? And where does she live?"

"She lives in Louisville, Kentucky. I've probably spent more than half my time up there in the past six months."

"Are you still splitting your time between here and there?"

"No. I told my mother I couldn't continue to spend weeks at a time up there. I'm a fashion designer, and I have commissions for a country music awards ceremony coming up in August."

"So you haven't been back to Louisville since—"

"Just over two weeks ago."

Banes raised his eyebrows. "And you bought a gun."

She nodded. His level gaze made her feel like a criminal. Her pulse sped up. He was going to ask her why she bought the gun, and right now she didn't have an answer to that question. She couldn't tell him the truth. She couldn't tell anyone. They'd label her a wacko.

"Why did you buy the gun, Resa?"

She looked down at her hands. "I don't know." To get close to Archer. To find out how he was coping with what the Lock Rapist had done. To ask him if he wanted to kill the rapist.

"Yes, you do."

She didn't look up. "I needed to protect myself."

Banes leaned back in his chair. She felt his eyes on her, felt his frown.

"Did you buy it because you'd noticed the car following you?"

She grimaced inwardly. "No. As I told you, the first time I noticed the car was two Tuesdays ago."

Banes made a note on his pad, then turned a couple of pages back. "The date on the gun's invoice was a week prior to that." He raised his gaze to hers. "So you bought a gun and a week later someone started following you. Can you explain that?"

"Is that how it happened?" She looked at her hands as she tried to remember what was going through her mind as she filled out the paperwork to purchase the gun.

"I came back from Louisville. My mother was mad at me for leaving her to cope with Celia alone. But my mother can be very stubborn. My sister needs to be in the hospital under a psychiatrist's care, but Mom won't hear of it."

She shook her head. "I understand Mom's point of view. Celia is her daughter. She ought to be able to take care of her. But—" Resa stopped, seeing the impatience in the detective's face.

"I'm sorry. I'm rambling. When I got back to Nashville, I was nervous about staying alone at night. So—"

Banes's eyes studied her. "You told me you'd never touched a gun before you bought the Glock."

"That's right."

His brow furrowed and his kind blue eyes sharpened. *He doesn't believe me.* What else could she say to convince him?

Just then she heard the front door open and close.

"Detective?"

"In here."

A young woman in jeans and T-shirt a with the letters CSU emblazoned across the front appeared at the door to the kitchen. *Crime Scene Unit.* "We're done here."

Banes nodded without taking his eyes off Resa. "Great. Has Impound been called?"

"Wait," Resa said. "You're impounding my car?"

"This is the closest we've ever gotten to the Lock Rapist. Your car is evidence."

"But—" She knew it would do no good to argue. But how was she going to work without her car? She'd lose her commissions—and probably her reputation.

Both Banes and the crime scene investigator looked at her.

"I'll—rent a car," she said meekly.

"Impound should be here within a few minutes, sir," the young woman said.

Banes nodded and turned his full attention back to Resa. "You were saying you'd never touched a gun before."

His tone made it clear that he knew she was hiding something.

She nodded.

"So how did you end up here?"

And here they were. Right where Clint Banes had been heading the whole time he'd been questioning her. It was the same question Archer had asked her. Why Archer's range?

"I heard about the range, and figured since it was owned by a former police detective, it would be a good place to learn to shoot."

"Yeah. I don't believe you, Ms. Wade."

A surge of fight-or-flight adrenaline heated her cheeks and neck. "Well, I'm sorry. It's the truth. I felt vulnerable, since the rapist probably saw my face that night. So I wanted to protect myself."

"Oh, that I believe. But you're lying about why you came here."

She felt her cheeks growing even hotter.

"Here's what I think. I think you are afraid of the Lock Rapist. You know he saw you, and you're afraid he's going to come after you." He paused and watched her for a few seconds.

Resa tried to stay calm, but the longer he was silent the more agitated she became. She felt as if he was looking right through her.

"I think you came here because you wanted to meet Geoff. You hoped he had a plan to go after the man who destroyed his life. You figured that's why he built the firing range. You were planning to be around when he caught the rapist. You want to be absolutely sure that he gets him. Then you can feel safe."

He leaned forward. "And you were shocked and disappointed when you found out that even after all this time, he can't shoot with his right hand."

A movement behind the detective caught Resa's eye. Archer was standing in the kitchen doorway. How long had he been there? "That's not why," she whispered.

But the damage was already done. Archer's eyes turned dark.

"Don't mind me," he said, stepping into the kitchen and heading for the refrigerator. "I just live here."

His voice dripped with bitterness.

Banes glanced in Archer's direction, but he kept talking to Resa. "You bought your gun not so you could protect yourself against the Lock Rapist. I think you bought it to use as a reason to come here. You wanted to be here when Geoff caught the rapist. You wanted him to exact the revenge you didn't think you could."

"I didn't—"

"Your glimpse of the Lock Rapist that night was kept out of the papers. So he had no way of knowing who you were, except as the latest victim's sister. You're the one who said he didn't start following you until after you showed up here."

"But that means—"

"He's been watching Geoff."

Resa's blood ran cold. "Then he saw me coming

to and from here." She intertwined her fingers together in her lap. "He saw me and recognized me."

"I think that's exactly what happened."

Archer moved on the edge of her vision. He opened a bottle of water and leaned against the kitchen counter, openly eavesdropping.

Detective Banes shot him a glowering look, but to Resa's surprise, he didn't tell him to leave.

"But why? Why was he watching Archer?"

"I think he's obsessed with him. When Geoff took over the case, he shut down the media coverage. Like many serial offenders, our guy craved the attention."

"And that's why he went after Archer's wife."

Detective Banes nodded.

"But why is he still watching him? Why didn't he turn to you when you took over the case?"

"Hey, I'm supposed to be asking the questions."

"Oh, that's right." She smiled at him. As probing as his questions were, he was kind and considerate. He was obviously very good at putting people at ease. She looked at Archer then back at him. What a difference between the two men.

Banes could coax a suspect into a feeling of security. Then, when the suspect got friendly and talkative, Archer could swoop in for the kill.

They must have been formidable together.

"Still, I'll try to answer your question. I think that's what obsession is. The rational thing—if anything a person like this does can be called rational—would be to transfer the blame to whoever is in the line of fire.

In this case, the new lead detective on the case. But this guy apparently is fixated on Geoff. I have a feeling nothing short of killing Geoff would satisfy his need for revenge."

Archer didn't say a word, but his face grew darker and darker.

"And since you showed up at the range, you've become part of his obsession. I have no doubt that he'd use you if he could to lure Geoff into his trap. Which is why I want to get you out of here as soon as possible."

Archer straightened. "Hold on, Clint. I thought you said you didn't have anybody to guard her."

Resa glanced at him. Another reminder that he'd only agreed to let her stay here because he had no other choice.

"I will have someone within the next couple of days," Clint shot at Archer, then turned back to her.

"Okay. Listen to me. You stay here. Do not go anywhere alone. Don't leave the house unless Geoff is with you. Understand?"

She nodded. "But why would he come after me? It doesn't make sense. Archer told me about the type of woman he targets. I'm totally not his type—I'm nothing like my sister or the other victims."

Banes rubbed his chin. "Like I said, he's obsessed with Geoff. He attacked his wife in retaliation for cutting off his media attention. If he thinks Geoff cares for you, then you will be his next victim."

Chapter Six

Earl took a long swig of beer and opened another bag of pretzels. He was sitting at his kitchen table, gloating to himself over how easy it was to manipulate people. He'd slipped the note into Theresa Wade's car in only a couple of seconds. His only regret was that he hadn't been able to hang around to watch her find the note.

He closed his eyes and took another swig of beer. She'd probably looked around to see if she could spot anyone leaving the area.

He'd waited on a side street to see what she would do. He speculated on her actions. His best guess had been that she'd call Archer. If she did that, Archer would call the police and Earl would soon have heard sirens.

But she'd surprised him. Within five minutes, she drove out of the subdivision alone. He didn't want her to see him. He wanted her to be *terrified* that she would see him.

Now he was ready to put his next step into motion. He wanted to spook not only Theresa, but Archer, too.

He grinned and stuffed his mouth full of pretzels. This got better and better every day. He had his plan ready. When the time was right, he would make an anonymous phone call to Archer's day manager, Frank Berry. What better way to mess with Archer than to give him more than one person to worry about?

As soon as Archer got the call from Frank and headed over to his house, Earl would case Archer's place. He needed information on how to get close to his house without being seen. He needed to be familiar with the safest and straightest course from his car to Archer's house and back. It was all about avoiding risk while satisfying the inferno that raged inside him.

But this time, it was also about pleasure—pleasure Earl had never realized could be his. He'd never played with his victims like this before. He'd never had time. In the past, he'd been forced to juggle his work with the days his wife and kids were out of town. He'd had to carefully plan his time in order to be able to take care of the burning before his family got home.

This time was lots better. Fun. Jerking folks around like puppets was a huge turn-on for him. Almost better than attacking the women.

Almost.

RESA BENT OVER the little cotton top and pushed the needle through a turquoise bead, added two rhinestones and a silver bead, then secured them to the neckline.

There. The last one. She leaned back in the desk chair and arched her neck to take the stiffness out, just as a knock sounded on her door.

"Resa?" Archer's voice carried through the closed wooden door.

"Come in."

He pushed the door open. "Everything all right?"

"Sure," she said. "Why? Has something happened?"

He shook his head. "I just hadn't seen you all morning."

"All morning?" She looked at the clock on the mantel of the unused fireplace. "Oh, it's almost noon."

"I noticed you'd gotten a cup of coffee earlier, but I thought maybe you'd gone back to sleep."

"I'm finishing this outfit for my client. Although I'm sure she'll want me to change it."

"Clint called a few minutes ago."

Resa sat up straight. "Has he got something?"

"Yeah. They got a partial print from the back of the note he left in your car. No matches though."

"It's not mine, is it? I tried to be careful but—"

He shook his head. "It's not yours. He's had it run against the only other print we've recovered so far— a full clear print left on a bedroom window latch."

"So that's what the other evidence you mentioned is. Another fingerprint. Where was it? Which victim?"

"My wife." Pain flashed in his eyes but it was gone instantly. "The window had an intricate lock. We figure he must have had to take off his gloves to work it."

Resa clamped her jaw. She should have expected that. That's why he hadn't wanted to discuss the other evidence. She should have known better than to ask. Now, perversely, she wanted to know more—more about what had happened on the night his wife was attacked. What had happened the day his wife shot him and then turned the gun on herself?

She took a deep breath. "Those intricate locks— they're on this house?"

He shook his head. "We lived in a town house. I bought this place...afterward, partly because of the huge basement. It had been empty for years. It still needs a lot of work."

She nodded. He hadn't wanted to stay in the house where his wife had died. She understood. She'd moved as soon as she could from the apartment where her sister had been attacked.

"I'm really sorry about your wife."

"Yeah. Me, too."

Resa felt her eyes sting as she watched Archer struggle to maintain his neutral expression. He worked so hard to pretend that nothing affected him.

But it did. It was obvious. Even when he smiled, he made her want to cry.

She stood and took the top she'd just finished over to her dressmaker's form, where a long suede skirt hung low on the form's hips. She put the top on the form and stood back.

"Not much to that top," he said, eyeing the huge gap between the bottom edge of the top and the top of the skirt. Resa gathered up some material at the back of the top and folded it together, then pinned it with a straight pin.

"Archer, do you think it's a coincidence that he left a nice perfect fingerprint at *your* house? I mean, as careful as he's been, it's kind of hard to believe that he'd slip up on the one job that would draw the most attention."

Archer leaned against the door facing and crossed his arms. "I wondered about that at the time. Wondered if he was so arrogant, so confident, that he'd risk leaving such an important clue just to taunt me. But every victim has described him as wearing gloves, and there were marks on the window hardware where someone had wiped the surface with a cloth."

He straightened and nodded at the clock. "Clint wants to show you a photo-array of various grilles and headlights of cars. He wants you to go through them, see if you can pick out the car that followed you."

"He offered to let me do that when I first called him."

"And you didn't?"

"I wasn't sure how much good it would do, and I was angry and scared that the police didn't care that I was being followed. Do you think it'll do any good?"

"It'll be a start. We might be able to get the make of the car. It depends on how unique the front grille and lights are. If it's a Mercedes, it'll be easy to identify. If it's a GM model, well, many of their vehicles have a family resemblance in the shape of the headlights and grille."

She nodded. "So it's another long shot."

"We'll get him, Resa. Piece by piece. That's how evidence works."

"He's been out there three years. When do you think you'll have something other than a long shot? What about the partial print? Did it match the full?"

He shook his head. "One was a finger and one a thumb. Hard to tell."

"The prints don't match anyone in the files?"

"Fingerprint evidence isn't as easy as the TV shows make it look. There is a database kept by the FBI, but for the most part the only people whose fingerprints are on file are government employees, military personnel and criminals. An ordinary guy with an ordinary job has probably never been printed."

"You aren't telling me that the Lock Rapist is an ordinary guy."

"To everyone in his everyday world he is a normal guy. He's got a wife and kids, a job that pays well and is steady but is beneath his intelligence level, and when his neighbors find out what he's done, they'll all say they can't believe he's a rapist. He was always so nice and quiet."

RESA DIDN'T get very far with identifying the car that had been following her. They finally narrowed it down to a mid-sized Ford product. Based on the shape of the headlights and the width and length of the grille, Archer figured it was probably a Taurus, several years old.

By the time she and Archer got back to his house,

she was hot and tired and grouchy, and so was he. They hadn't spoken on the car ride home.

Archer closed the front door then unlocked the door to the living room for her.

"I'm going down to talk to Frank about opening the outdoor range."

"Outdoor range? Where's that?"

He pressed his lips together impatiently. "It's around back. For shooting longer targets and more powerful weapons than we can handle downstairs. The indoor range is only twenty-five yards."

"Oh." None of what he was saying made a whole lot of sense to her except that the outdoor range was much bigger than the one in the basement. "Um, why hasn't it already been open?"

"Because we just finished it. A lot of the guys on the force want a bigger range to practice on."

She nodded. "They don't shoot toward the house, do they?" she said in a gently teasing voice.

He frowned at her for a second. Then his eyes crinkled just a little at the corners. "No. Not usually."

"Good to know."

He nodded and wiped his mouth. She'd like to think he was wiping away a smile, but that might be too much to hope for.

"I'm going to take a shower, if that's all right with you."

Archer scowled at her. "Of course it's all right with me."

"Where should I go when I'm done? I wouldn't

want to surprise you in the basement while you're shooting."

Any hint of teasing was gone from his face. She'd gone too far and angered him. "You can go wherever the hell you want to go. In fact, maybe you ought to come downstairs. I thought you wanted me to teach you how to shoot."

Resa cocked her head at Archer. "You know—I'd love that. But I've gotten the very definite impression you'd prefer not to have me anywhere near you or your range—either of your ranges. Maybe I'll ask Frank to teach me."

"*I'll* teach you. Bring your weapon and your ammunition downstairs when you're ready."

AFTER A QUICK shower, Resa felt a lot better. She put on a pair of soft linen pants and a white sleeveless top. With a touch of lip gloss and her damp hair in a ponytail, she was ready.

Down in the firing range, Archer had changed into jeans and a T-shirt and was sitting at his desk, his forearms on his knees, squeezing a hand exerciser with his right hand.

He didn't notice her at first, so she watched him. His biceps and the muscles in his forearms flexed with each squeeze. But pain was etched into the corners of his mouth and eyes, and into the sculpted line of his jaw.

She could tell his hand wasn't working right. It took him too much effort to press the individual finger keys, and his index finger hardly worked at all.

"If you're so curious, come closer."

She jumped. "I—I'm sorry—" she stammered. "You were concentrating so—"

He looked up at her from under his brows. "Why so fascinated? Afraid I'm not capable of protecting you?"

"No. I just—" Could she tell him she ached to see him hurting so much? That her fascination was with his single-minded determination, his dogged effort to fix his hand that she was terribly afraid wasn't fixable?

He tossed the hand exerciser onto his desk and joined her at the door, massaging his palm. "Did you bring your weapon?"

"It's in my purse."

"You remember I told you Glocks don't have a safety? Carrying it loose in your purse is a dangerous practice. Something could lodge in the trigger pull and the gun could go off accidentally. I'd hate to see you shoot yourself." He slid past her, his T-shirt brushing her bare arm, and headed down to lane ten.

She followed, finding it difficult to keep up with his long strides. "So how should I carry it?"

"Either get a purse holster or a paddle holster, which goes back here." He turned and placed his hand on her back, spreading his fingers just below her waist and just above the swell of her hips.

She suppressed a shiver. The speed at which he removed his hand made her think he'd felt it, too.

"Maybe I'll get both. It seems like it would be nice to have more than one choice."

He gently grasped her shoulders and placed her in the very center of the narrow cubicle. "Give that some thought. It's not a good idea to have too many different places to keep your weapon. You don't want to be reaching for the wrong place when your life is at stake."

He stood behind her, his hands still on her shoulders as she retrieved her gun and the box of ammunition from her purse.

He talked her through the ritual of inspecting her weapon and loading it. Then he handed her the ear protectors and goggles. Once she'd donned them, he rested his hands lightly on her upper arms.

"Now spread your legs."

The words were muffled through the ear protectors. It took her a fraction of a second to absorb what he'd said. When she did, her whole body went rigid. Something about the drowsy warm feeling of her shower combined with his careful touches and the sexy innuendo of his words had her weak as a schoolgirl in the throes of her first crush.

Archer slid his hands down her arms and shifted them to either side of her waist. "Come on. Bring your legs about two feet apart and balance."

He was doing it on purpose. He had to be—with his firm yet gentle fingers and his low compelling voice. There was absolutely nothing sexy about learning to shoot a gun. Was he trying to intimidate her? Embarrass her? Make her run away?

Archer spread his fingers around her waist, cursing

himself for giving in to the urge to touch her. If he had any sense, he'd let Frank teach her to shoot. He didn't want to be here. Didn't want his head filled with her fresh melony scent, or his hands filled with her firm, supple flesh. He let go.

"Are you balanced?"

She nodded.

"Good, because if you lose your footing while you're shooting it could be deadly. Now raise the gun."

She awkwardly lifted the gun to shoulder height.

His hands hovered millimeters from her bare arms, so close he could feel the heat of her skin. "What did I tell you about holding the gun? Use both hands. You throw yourself off balance when you use just one hand."

"It still feels awkward," she said. "Maybe the gun is too heavy for me."

"It's not too heavy. You're afraid of it. You have to master it. That doesn't mean you don't respect it and what it can do. But if you're afraid to use your weapon properly, you'll end up in more danger than if you were unarmed."

He moved up close behind her, pressing against her and reaching around to take her wrists in his hands. "Relax," he rasped. Then he had to suppress a laugh at himself.

Relax, hell. He was wrapped around her like a lover and fighting his body's response to the almost forgotten, seductive feel of a woman.

He swallowed and concentrated on positioning her

arms correctly. "Grip the gun in your right hand and support it with your left as you raise it."

Her movements were jerky, her muscles tense.

"Come on, Resa. Loosen up." He ran his palms up her arms and back down. *Damn.* Her skin felt like velvet.

"Try to raise the gun in a fluid movement. One continuous motion." He held her right wrist and her left forearm—not hard, just enough to urge them gently upward.

"Keep your left arm bent, use that hand like a gun rest. It supports your gun hand." He bent his head close to her ear protector. "Now squeeze the trigger."

He felt her arms tense, felt her tension all the way up into her shoulders. He watched her index finger as she tightened it on the trigger.

When the gun went off, the recoil pushed her backward, into him. She dropped the gun onto the countertop and yanked off the goggles and ear protectors and tossed them down beside it. "I can't do this."

She turned around and Archer saw dampness glistening in her eyes.

"You're too stiff—"

"No. That's not it. I can't do anything with you wrapped around me like that. I can't think of anything but—" Her cheeks turned bright pink and she ducked her head. "Never mind."

Warning bells clanged in his head. This was dangerous ground. He should turn around and leave. Go back into his office and put his desk between himself and her distracting body.

But he knew he wasn't going to do that. It was too late. He'd passed the point of no return.

He'd sworn to protect her and instead he'd let himself think of things—dream of things—that shouldn't matter to him.

The love of his life had died. He had no business thinking of another woman—especially not this woman, and certainly not this soon.

To his dismay, he realized she wasn't going to drop the subject. She raised her head and met his gaze. "You don't feel it, do you?"

He couldn't make his vocal cords work.

She put her fingers over her mouth and shook her head. "I'm sorry. I'm making an idiot out of myself. I'll get Frank to—"

"Resa." He wrapped his fingers around her wrist and pulled her hand away from her mouth. "I heard what Clint said to you. He's right. You have some misguided notion that if you're close to me, I can help you get revenge on the Lock Rapist for hurting your sister." He stared into her dark-green eyes, seeing himself reflected there.

No, not himself. A glorified version of himself. A whole man. A hero.

His heart ached. As much as he'd like to be that man, he knew he wasn't—knew he'd never be.

She moistened her lips and desire raged through him, totally inappropriate and completely uncontrollable.

"Don't expect me to help you, Resa. I can't. I can't

even help myself. It's all I can do to get through the day."

She raised her hand and touched his cheek, a featherlight glide of her fingertips along his skin and down the tense line of his jaw. "You do want him, don't you? You'd do anything to catch him."

He bent his head until his forehead touched hers. The truth scraped like a rasp across his throat. "I'd kill him if I could."

She pressed her palms against his chest, her heat branding their imprint into his skin.

"I want to be there beside you," she whispered. "I want to kill him, too."

He shook his head, rubbing his forehead against hers. "No, you don't. You don't want blood on your hands."

"My sister's blood is already on my hands."

"God, Resa, don't talk that way." He pulled her into his arms, his hand cupping the back of her head and his nose buried in her hair.

Resa wrapped her arms around Archer's lean waist. He felt just as she'd known he would. Hard, strong, unyielding. Like a hero.

He blew out a shaky breath, stirring her hair and tickling her ear. She slid her hand up to encircle the back of his neck. As she did, he shifted and she felt the hard ridge of his erection through the stiff denim of his jeans.

Longing spiraled through her all the way to her sexual center. Her thighs tightened and she arched toward him, craving the sensation of his hard body against hers.

Her lips skimmed his unshaven cheek as she searched for his mouth. He lifted his head slightly. Their lips met.

Resa felt faint. Her senses reeled at the feel of his kiss. His mouth was firm, his jaw rock-hard, but his lips were surprisingly gentle as they moved over hers.

Too soon he stopped and rested his chin on top of her head. "We can't do this," he whispered raggedly.

"I know," she mouthed against his collarbone, believing him, agreeing with him, but unable to move away from him.

"We're just lonely." He slid his palms up her arms to her shoulders. "We're just seeking comfort."

She nodded. "Comfort—" She reached for his mouth.

He kissed her again, this time more sweetly, softly, heartbreakingly. Then he pulled away, leaving his forearms resting on her shoulders. He hung his head and spoke in a muffled tone.

"I'm empty, Resa. There's nothing left inside me. You'll end up hating me."

"I won't." But his words were ominous. Did he really believe he had nothing to give? What if he were right? What if he was nothing more than an empty shell?

She couldn't believe that. She'd seen his grief, his anger, his cold determination. And now she'd seen his gentleness.

Could she convince him he was wrong?

She put her palms on his cheeks and urged his head up.

He squeezed his eyes closed, as if he couldn't bear to look at her.

"I could never hate you. You are too honorable. Too noble. Admit it, Archer, you feel something. Tell me you feel at least a little of what I feel. We need each other. We can make each other stronger—"

A banging echoed through the house.

Resa jerked, and Archer whirled on the balls of his feet.

"What's that?" she asked.

"Someone's at the door. Are you expecting anyone?"

She shook her head. "No one knows where I am."

"Give me your gun," he commanded.

"Why? Who do you think it is?"

"I don't know. That's why I want your gun."

She handed it over.

Archer gripped it in his left hand as he stepped out of the cubicle. "Stay here," he snapped when she moved to follow him.

"What are you going to do? Should I call 911?"

He silenced her with a glare. "Just wait. It could be nothing."

Archer cautiously approached the stairs. As he did he heard the lock on the front door rattle. He flipped on the lights and vaulted up the stairs to the foyer. As he got closer, the banging sounded more like a fist pounding on the door.

He gripped the little Glock awkwardly in his left hand, and aimed it at the front door. "Who is it?"

The pounding stopped.

"Geoff! It's me! Frank. Open up."

Archer unlocked the door and opened it. Frank was standing there, his face nearly as white as his hair.

"Frank. What the hell?"

"I got a voice message." He held out his cell phone. "I didn't want to call you in case he called back."

"Who? Get in here."

Archer motioned Frank inside and took a quick look around the front of the house before he closed and locked the door.

"Listen to this." Frank's hands shook as he entered the code to play the voice message.

"Hello, Frank. You might want to check on your boss. He and his pretty little house guest are in danger."

Archer's scalp burned as he listened to the honey-smooth voice. It was the Lock Rapist. He knew it. But why would he call Frank?

"Has something happened? Are you and Resa all right?" Frank asked, wiping sweat off his upper lip.

Archer shook his head. "We're fine."

Resa appeared at the bottom of the stairs. "Frank! I thought I heard your voice. What's wrong?"

"I told you to stay put." Archer tossed a frown in her direction, then turned back to his friend, an awful thought forming in his brain. "Frank, where's Linda?"

"She's at the house. Why?" Then understanding dawned on Frank's face. "Oh my God! My wife! She's there alone."

Chapter Seven

"I've got to call my wife, get her out of the house."
Frank grabbed for his cell phone.

"Hold on." Archer pocketed Frank's phone and retrieved his own. Frank's phone was evidence. "I don't
want her leaving the house. He might be waiting for
her. We need to call the police. They can be there in
a couple of minutes." He dialed 911 and gave them
the address. Then he called Clint.

"Clint. There may be trouble at Frank's house. I've
called 911."

He glanced at Frank. "Stay here with Resa. I'm
going over there."

"Hell no!" Frank cried. "I'm not waiting around
here."

"All right. I'll follow you. Resa, let's go. We're
taking a drive." Archer headed out the door and
jumped into his car. As soon as Resa got in, he sped
down the driveway behind Frank.

He didn't know what the Lock Rapist was up to,

calling Frank and luring him out of his home, but no matter what his scheme was, Archer wasn't about to let him get away with it. He was an idiot if he thought Archer would run off and leave Resa behind.

"What's he doing?" Resa asked, as Archer whipped his car around behind two black-and-whites parked in front of Frank's house with a their blue lights strobing.

He knew who she was talking about.

He shook his head. "Trying to scare us. Trying to prove he can manipulate us. Maybe trying to get us out of the house."

Frank shot out of his car as if he'd been shot from a cannon. He pushed past two uniformed officers and sprinted toward his house.

Archer started to follow him. But the front door opened and Frank's wife was standing there. She gawked in surprise at all the police cars.

Frank grabbed her in a bear hug. She was fine.

Clint walked up. "Looks like everything's okay."

Archer didn't comment. He wasn't so sure. "Make sure you get Frank's cell phone. There's a recorded message on it from the Lock Rapist."

Clint raised his eyebrows. "Oh yeah? How'd he get Frank's number?"

"It's listed as a second number for the range in the phone book."

"So what was the point of all this?"

"I've got no clue what he was trying to accomplish. But whatever his reasoning, it made sense to him. I tell you what Clint. I'm going to close the ranges until all this is over. I don't like the idea of involving Frank and his wife."

"That's probably a good idea. You can keep a better eye on Resa, too, if you don't have folks wandering around your house and grounds."

"Yeah."

"I don't like any of this. What's happening to this guy? It seems to me he's veering way off profile. What he's doing now feels less like a serial offender and more like a vendetta."

Archer nodded grimly. "I know. And that means we can't predict what he's going to do next."

RESA COULDN'T sleep. She looked at the clock. It was after midnight. She couldn't get Frank's terrified face out of her mind. Or Archer's grim resolve.

She'd known when he'd come in and told Frank everything was fine, that he was lying.

Oh, Frank and Linda were safe. He'd promised Frank that, and she knew that what Archer promised, he delivered.

After they'd left Frank's and gone home, Archer had been in no mood to talk. He'd sent her a level gaze and told her to go to bed. When she tried to protest, wanting to know everything that had happened, he stopped her.

"We'll be up early," he'd said. "We've got to go in and see what Clint has uncovered."

So with the promise of hearing about the evidence,

she'd come upstairs and climbed into bed. But she'd tossed and turned until the bed was a mess and she was nervous as a cat. Finally, she kicked the tangled covers away from her feet and got up.

Her dress form, with the suede skirt and the midriff top, stood like a silent ghost in the corner of the room. Often when she couldn't sleep, she'd work on her designs, but tonight she was too antsy.

All she had left to do on Chastity's outfit were the final embellishments and trim. Then she'd be done with it. She held her trembling hands out in front of her. If she tackled the intricate beadwork tonight, she'd ruin the whole outfit.

Instead she decided to slip downstairs to the kitchen and get a glass of milk, or herb tea if Archer had any. Maybe then she could get a few hours' sleep.

She slipped through the door to the hall and quietly closed it. She couldn't help but glance at Archer's bedroom door. It was closed. He must be having better luck sleeping than she was.

She crept silently down the stairs and through the living room into the kitchen. The light over the stove was on, serving as a night-light.

A quick perusal of the kitchen cabinets uncovered an unopened basket of herb teas—obviously a gift at some time. When she took the twist-tie off the cellophane, it crackled loudly and the edges crumpled in her fingers. Archer had probably never voluntarily drunk herb tea in his life, nor would he.

Smiling a little at the idea of his sipping chamomile

tea from a porcelain cup, she filled the kettle with water and put it on to heat.

Within a couple of minutes she was standing at the window over the sink, sipping her tea. She hadn't paid attention to Archer's backyard. But tonight, with the low light from over the stove and the bright moonlight, she could see the outdoor shooting range that he'd mentioned the other day. In the moonlight the cast-iron targets were silhouetted against the sky like weird shadow-people. Behind them, hills of dirt provided a backstop for bullets.

The house and grounds were fraught with layers and contradictions, a lot like Archer himself. Looking at the house from the front, it appeared to be an immaculate, manicured Victorian mansion. No one would guess it hid a dangerous, potentially deadly cavern underneath it, or a massive outdoor shooting range behind it.

In the same way, looking at Archer when he was cleaned up, with creased trousers, starched shirt, clean-shaven cheeks and neatly combed hair, it was hard to believe he was the same person as the haunted, shadowed creature in worn jeans and faded T-shirt who prowled in the darkness and dared anyone to approach him.

Both sides of him fascinated her, but which was the real Geoffrey Archer? She had no idea.

EARL SLATTERY'S innards quivered in excitement as he watched Theresa through Archer's kitchen window. As she leaned slightly forward to fill the copper kettle with water, the little pajama thing she wore gaped, giving him an excellent look at her boobs.

Just the sight of her got his nature up. There was no accounting for it. She wasn't anything like the little blondes he was drawn to. But she was definitely hot, and she looked like a fighter.

He squirmed, imagining her struggling uselessly against him while he tormented her. He wasn't big and tall like Archer, but he was strong. Strong enough to make any woman do whatever he wanted her to.

He had to take care of Theresa Wade—fast. She'd looked right at him that night. He should have gone after her then, but it was too risky. And Earl didn't take risks—not if he could help it.

But now she was consorting with Archer. She'd even moved into his house. Maybe they thought people would believe it was so he could protect her. But Earl knew. She was a whore, just like his mother.

"Oh, no! Sorry, Mom," he whispered. "I didn't mean to think that. I know you had to make money somehow. I love you." He took a deep, steadying breath. "Guess what, Mommy? I'll be ready soon, and you'll be so proud. I'll be on TV again. They'll all be talking about me."

The idea of being in the paper and on the TV news again magnified the burning. It swelled up inside him until he thought he would burst with it. He shut his eyes and gave himself up to it for a few exhilarating seconds.

He knew the inferno was leading him in the right direction, to Theresa Wade. It was the perfect way to get rid of her and destroy Archer all over again. Once he took care of her, let Archer try to keep him out of the news.

The reporters would be all over it—the Lock Rapist doing Archer's woman not once but twice.

Earl squirmed. His plans had him so worked up, but he couldn't do anything about it right now. He had to get away from here and cover his tracks.

The cops who had cruised around Archer's place earlier might come back. His phone call to Archer's range manager had worked better than he'd hoped.

Archer had dropped everything and headed out to check on Berry's wife. He'd called his police buddies to check out Berry's house and his own.

Once the police vehicle had made a cursory check of Archer's place and left, Earl was able to drive around without fear of being noticed. He'd already used the Internet to map out the farm roads around Archer's acreage. One ran fairly close to Archer's house. It took Earl only a few minutes to sneak across the fields and wooded areas until he had a great view of Archer's back porch and his kitchen window.

Catching Theresa at the window, dressed for bed, had been a bonus.

But now the moon was up and pale light illuminated the field. He'd probably seen all there was to see tonight. As Theresa turned away from the window, Earl slowly backed away from his vantage point.

Then a shadow moved behind her. *Archer.*

Earl's pulse sped up and sweat stung his armpits and his back. He couldn't leave now. It looked like the show was just starting.

"Everything okay?"

Resa was so immersed in her thoughts of him that for a few seconds she didn't realize his raspy voice was real and not a part of her fantasy.

She half turned and angled her head. His bare feet were in her line of vision. They were long, strong feet, with sexy toes and a high, defined arch. Blue-striped pajama pants hid his ankles.

She turned around and allowed her gaze to slide up his pants' legs to the drawstring waist that rode low on his hips. He didn't have on a shirt. His belly and hips looked as lean and hard as they'd felt under her fingers. His chest was as broad, his shoulders as wide and defined. He was thinner than he looked in clothes, but at the same time, he was also more cut.

"Resa?"

She blinked. "Oh." Her face burned. How long had she been staring at his body? "I'm sorry—"

"What's wrong?" He frowned.

She shook her head. "Nothing. I couldn't sleep." Her fingers tightened around the cup. "Do you want some tea?"

"Tea?"

She forced herself to focus on his eyes. He was looking at her hands. She blinked. No, he wasn't. He was looking at *her.* At the lace edge of her little satin camisole. Feeling his hot gaze on her barely covered breasts made them tighten in response.

The cup was warm in her hands, reminding her of the warmth of his lips against hers.

Oh, she had to stop this.

"Tea," she repeated. "It's chamomile." She swallowed nervously. "Good for calming—things."

His eyes lit with amusement. "Calming things? Then yes. I could use some things calmed."

It was all she could do to keep from looking down at the front of his pajamas. She felt her face turning pink, so she turned away toward the stove. Setting down her cup she picked up a mug and poured him some hot tea. She slid the mug across the counter in his direction.

"Sugar?"

He wrapped his fingers around the mug, ignoring the handle. Shaking his head, he took a sip. "Chamomile, eh?"

"You're laughing at me."

"Not really. More at the situation." He blew on the steaming liquid. "I'll talk to Clint first thing in the morning. Surely by now he can free up somebody to guard you."

So that was it. He didn't know how to act, now that they'd kissed. She knew he wasn't happy with himself or her. And she couldn't blame him.

On the other hand, she couldn't be sorry for what they'd done either. He might be still in love with his dead wife, but she had no ties, no tragic love in her past. She could count on one hand—hell on one finger—the times she'd ever been swept off her feet by a single kiss. This was it.

For him, it might have been a mistake, a regret he wanted to erase, but for her, those few moments of closeness were something she'd treasure forever. Geoffrey Archer was the most compelling man she'd ever met. How could she say he didn't matter?

She was seriously afraid that to her, he mattered much more than one person ever should to another.

She looked up from her hands to find him watching her, a bewildered expression on his face.

She nodded and forced a smile. "Good," she said. "That's probably good. Someone to guard me. Of course. I'm sure you're ready for me to be out of here." She took a step backward.

He set his mug down and stepped toward her. "You're right." His eyes grew dark. "In a lot of ways I do wish you weren't here."

Resa felt compelled to move backward again. She took another step back and found herself pressed against the big porcelain sink, her back to the window. His penetrating gaze held her in thrall as her brain replayed what he'd just said.

A lot of ways? What did that mean?

He took her cup out of her numb hands and set it away from them on the counter.

"I can be gone tomorrow."

He shook his head.

"Yes. I'll talk to Clint when we go in to see him tomorrow. My car should be ready, too."

"No."

His stern look and terse answers confused her. Hadn't he just said he wished she were gone? He moved closer, sending her heart rate sky-high. What was he doing? His body language was sending a totally different message from his words.

"Well, I'd better get to bed." She pushed away from the sink, expecting Archer to get out of her way.

He didn't.

She ran into that rock-hard body and his arms shot out to steady her.

There was very little of anything between them. Just the thin cotton of her camisole. Her breasts were already tight and aching. She moaned quietly as their sensitized tips scraped against the hairs on his chest. The unmistakable ridge of his hardness pressed against her belly, sending thrills of longing throbbing through her.

She splayed her fingers across his chest, lightly brushing his nipples. She felt them harden beneath her touch. At the same time, his erection pulsed. The fact that he was turned on by her touch made her knees weak with desire.

When she looked up, his dark gaze was soft with passion, but also wary. His chest rose and fell with strong, quick breaths.

He let go of her arms and put his hands over hers. She took a deep breath, expecting him to push her away, but he didn't. Instead he guided her hands down and around his waist. His skin was like hot silk, stretched taut over the hard planes of his muscles.

He ducked his head, like a kid trying to work up courage to ask for a date. She leaned close enough to rub her nose against his.

He looked up and she let her lips barely graze his, waiting to see what he would do.

His inner struggle was palpable. She understood his warring emotions. In the five months since her sister's rape, she'd withdrawn, afraid to trust. All her time and concentration had been consumed with the need to mete out justice to the man who'd destroyed her sister's life.

How much stronger must Archer's need be? Because of the Lock Rapist, he'd lost his wife twice— first when she'd been raped, then the ultimate loss when she'd killed herself.

"Resa," he whispered raggedly against her mouth. "You don't want to do this."

She hesitated. Was he right? His body hot against hers and his desperate effort to hold himself in control fed her yearning.

She nodded. "Yes, I do."

Their bodies were pressed so tightly together that she knew when he gave in. She felt his arms relax, felt the spring-loaded tension in his shoulders and back loosen a bit.

His hands slid along her forearms, past her elbows and up. Then he bent and kissed her shoulder, right on its bony curve. The kiss sent currents of erotic fire straight to her sexual center.

She slid her hands up and encircled his neck, kissing him with passion, with abandon.

He spanned her waist with his hands and pulled her even closer as he returned her kiss. He trailed his mouth and tongue down the side of her neck and on to her collarbone. His hands slid upward, pushing her top out of the way. He gasped when his thumbs brushed the underside of her breasts.

At his touch, her body arched toward him. She caressed the swell of his buttocks. She touched the drawstring waist of his pajama pants.

He took a sharp breath. "Wait," he said hoarsely. Then he lifted her with no effort and sat her on the edge of the sink.

She gasped as the cold porcelain pressed into her backside.

He spread her legs and ran his hands over her inner thighs. She strained toward his questing fingers, already too close to losing control. She melted under his touch. Her insides turned to liquid heat.

Everything grew dark. For an instant Resa thought her eyes had hazed over with desire. Then she realized a cloud had obscured the pale light of the moon.

The absurdity of their position slammed into her hazy brain. She was practically naked, perched in front of a window, exposed.

"Archer, wait. Please."

He froze, but didn't remove his hands. After a few seconds, he slid his fingers farther up her thighs, skimming the edge of her panties.

"No, please."

He straightened. "Sorry," he muttered on a sigh.

She caught his forearm as he turned away. "Take me upstairs. I can't do this here." She gestured.

"You want to—"

She nodded, moistening her lips and pushing her fingers through her hair. "But I want to do it right—you know—romantically." She felt her cheeks burn. "Not like this."

He brushed the backs of his fingers gently across her hot cheek. "You know what? Me, too."

OUTSIDE, watching through the window, Earl licked his lips and adjusted his pants, squirming in acute discomfort. The play that had unfolded in front of him suddenly came to a halt.

Archer lifted Theresa down from her wanton perch on the sink and led her away from the window. Earl could imagine what they were doing. He figured they were going upstairs to one of the bedrooms.

Sure enough, within seconds their silhouettes appeared through the windows on the second story. As they came into view, Archer turned toward her and kissed her without touching her. Then he took her hand. They disappeared again, only to reappear in front of the double windows at the west corner of the house.

There they came together in a repeat of the urgent kisses they'd shared in the kitchen.

Earl watched them hungrily, relishing his discomfort, glorying in the inferno that boiled within him. Soon, though, his emotions were in turmoil. He hated

Archer. He wanted Theresa. It was torture, watching them together.

As their silhouettes moved away from the window—toward the bed, Earl was sure—he moaned deeply, a guttural wail.

He couldn't stand it anymore. He had to have relief. The burning was about to engulf his whole being. If he didn't do something soon, he would burst into flames.

Chapter Eight

Archer's room was dark, with only the light from the bathroom providing any illumination. His bed was unmade. The pillow still held the imprint of his head. The sheet and comforter were bunched at the foot of the bed.

He stopped beside the bed and tugged on her hand until she faced him. "Resa, this is not a good idea."

She gave him a tentative smile. "Isn't it?"

He shook his head. "I told you before. I have nothing to give you. You deserve better."

"Have I asked for anything?"

He frowned at her, holding her gaze. "I think so. I think you're asking for a hero, and that's not me."

"Stop it. You set too high a standard for yourself. Now shut up and kiss me."

He did. It started out tentative and ended up thorough and heart-stopping.

Then he tossed her onto the bed and followed her. With gentle, erotic movements he slid her camisole up and over her head. He coaxed her breasts into tight full arousal with his fingers, then bent his head and tongued and nipped at her nipples until the exquisite ache in her breasts traveled down to the center of her frantic desire.

Without a word, he slid his fingers past the elastic of her panties.

She gasped, so overwhelmed with sensation she couldn't catch her breath. She grabbed his wrist.

"Archer, please—" she begged breathlessly. "I can't hold out—"

"Then don't." His fingers inched downward until his fingertips brushed her bare skin. He stroked, lightly, gently, relentlessly. Any second now he'd discover just how close she was to losing it completely. She could feel the slick wetness he was about to encounter.

A part of her was embarrassed to be so easily aroused. But her womanly side overrode her rational side. She relaxed, opened up, welcomed his arousing touch. In another few seconds she was going to lose all control.

Archer felt her heat surrounding him as he stroked and dipped. Her summery melon scent engulfed him, stronger, sexier than he'd imagined. He kissed her again, plunging deeply and rhythmically with his tongue in an imitation of lovemaking. His fingers matched his tongue's rhythm as he urged her toward total release.

Then he felt them start—the tiny contractions that told him she was over the edge.

She moaned deep in her throat.

He never stopped his relentless stroking, coaxing her to greater and greater abandon. He watched her face, feeling a tender triumph when her eyes closed and her mouth opened.

Her entire body spasmed and he nearly came himself just watching her.

When she finally relaxed, boneless, against him, he tortured himself by pressing his pulsing hardness against her hip. The feeling was excruciatingly pleasurable. He leaned forward and kissed her mouth.

Her hands reached for the drawstring on his pajama pants. He nearly cried out when she brushed against his arousal as she pushed them down.

He kicked the pants off and raised himself above her, his weight on his forearms.

Her eyes opened. They were soft and dark, a deep mossy green. Languidly she slid her fingers over his biceps, up and around his shoulders, and down over his pecs. Her soft touches were like hot kisses on his skin, trailing erotic fire in their wake.

Then, just when he couldn't wait one more second for her to touch him, she reached between them and wrapped her hand around him. He shuddered and his erection pulsed against her palm.

She guided him. Her back arched and she moaned with pleasure as he entered her. The hot, slick sensation of sliding into her nearly pushed him over the edge. He panted, working to suppress the urge to sink to the hilt and allow himself to explode.

"Archer—now!" she cried, grasping his buttocks and arching upward, taking him deeper.

"I don't want to hurt—"

"Now!"

He gave himself up to the exquisite pleasure of her body. She matched his rhythm and his urgency. He couldn't wait, couldn't take it slow, but it didn't matter. She was right there with him, clenching around him, gasping with him, collapsing under him as he eased his weight onto her and buried his face in the curve of her neck and shoulder for a few seconds, before pulling away to lie beside her with her head resting on his shoulder.

Just as he drifted off to sleep, he thought about how much he was going to regret this when he woke up in the morning.

"WE'VE GOT another one."

It took Archer a second to understand what Clint was saying. He'd grabbed his cell phone before he was one hundred percent awake.

He sat up and swung his legs over the side of the bed. "What the hell?" he whispered. "Where?"

Clint gave him the details. "She's a single mother with one son, nine years old."

Archer cursed as he reached for his jeans. He stood, propping his cell phone awkwardly between his jaw and his shoulder as he pulled the jeans up over his backside. The phone slipped and he caught it just before it fell.

"Where are you? At the crime scene?"

"Just finishing up. The victim is on her way to the hospital. Why are you whispering?"

"I'm not whispering," he snapped. "Was there a lock of hair?"

"Yeah." Clint sounded as frustrated as Archer felt.

"What about the victim? Did she see anything? Can she identify him?" He already knew the answer to that question.

"Nope."

"I want to see the scene."

"No, Geoff. There's nothing to see. The crime scene people are almost done."

"What did they find? How did he get in?"

"Just like the others. No sign of forced entry. This vic had a security system, but it didn't go off."

"Damn it, there's got to be something. Something your guys missed." He looked over his shoulder. Resa was stirring. Her dark hair waved around her face. Her softly rounded shoulders and the swell of breasts barely hidden by the sheet sent a sharp thrill through him.

He grimaced. What an ass he was. He'd never intended to touch her. He'd sworn to himself that he wouldn't act on his irrational and totally inappropriate attraction.

Archer forced his attention back to Clint, who was talking.

"—think you can find something we missed? You processed three crime scenes yourself. Did you miss something in those?"

Resa sat up, pulling the sheet with her. He couldn't tear his eyes away from her. And he sure as hell couldn't think. He turned and stepped out into the hall, pulling the door closed behind him.

"I'm saying we've all missed something. It's the same old questions we've had since the beginning. Have you ever known a serial offender who was totally random?" He propped the phone between his shoulder and ear again, and managed to get the first couple of buttons on his jeans fastened, despite the cramping pain in his right hand.

"I'm just like you, Geoff. I've been in Nashville my whole career. This is the first serial case I've ever worked."

"That's my point. I think there's a connection between the victims that we've missed. Our guy has got to meet his victims somewhere. He's got to choose them somehow. He doesn't just walk down the street and spot a target. His attacks are all during the night. They're carefully planned. Meticulously organized."

"I know you checked all that. And I have, too. Every time. But I'll have my guys redo the background info and we'll take another look at the map. We never established his comfort zone, either, did we?"

"I'm coming down to the station. I haven't seen the map with all the victims pinpointed. I want to take look at it."

"Geoff—"

"Don't shut me out, Clint." He paced back and forth, pushing his fingers through his hair then rubbing the back of his neck. "I need to do this. I know there's a connection there—a clue. I've got to find it. The Lock Rapist is targeting Resa."

Archer turned off his phone and stared at his bedroom door. He'd screwed up big-time. He'd let Resa's sexy body and her trusting eyes get past his guard. He'd allowed himself to care, and he knew where that led—it led to mistakes, errors in judgment. It led to heartache. His job was to keep Resa safe, and he couldn't do that if his heart was involved.

EARL WOKE UP. His head hurt and his body felt as if he'd been on the wrong end of somebody's fist. He groaned and opened one matted eye to a narrow slit and took a careful breath. Dusty blue drapes. The smell of old grease. He was at home.

Relief relaxed his muscles and gave him the shakes. He turned over, groaning when the old couch's lumpy springs dug into his aching back and butt.

He threw an arm over his eyes and tried to go back to sleep. But his muscles were still twitching, and something else was wrong.

He coughed and stretched. In mid-yawn it hit him. *The burning!* It was gone!

Oh man oh man oh man oh man— His brain raced and every last muscle in his body convulsed in cramping spasms. He cried out as his chest contracted, cutting off his breath. He waited for his body to relax, waited to see if this would be the time his muscles betrayed him by squeezing the life out of him.

Finally he collapsed, his lungs greedily sucking in breath, his limbs like jelly after the vicious cramps.

He'd done it again—*and* gotten away with it.

He didn't know how long he lay there before he was able to drag himself up to a sitting position. He slumped forward, his head between his hands while dizziness engulfed him. As soon as he could focus, he looked down at himself. Sure enough, he had on the dark-blue coverall and black hooded jacket—his uniform for soothing the burning.

With trembling hands he unzipped the coverall and reached into the pocket of the pants he wore underneath. He sighed with relief as his fingers closed around his wallet. He dug it out and looked under the flap.

There it was. His precious envelope. He gingerly pulled out the ragged piece of paper. Inside was a brand-new lock of hair, as well as the remaining strands of the oldest lock he had. He touched them both reverently.

"I'm nearly done, Mommy." He held the envelope up to his nose. "I'm not going to last much longer. Watch for me. I'll be on the news. Mommy—I miss you. I'm so sorry. So sorry…so sorry."

Tucking the envelope back in its hiding place, he sniffed and rubbed his eyes.

He pulled himself up the stairs, leaning heavily on the banister because his legs were still too shaky to hold him up. He had to hide his clothes and shower.

Just as he reached the top of the stairs, a memory

hit him like a punch to the gut. Theresa, standing at Archer's window in her little pajama top. Archer coming up behind her. The two of them kissing, then disappearing only to reappear as silhouettes upstairs in Archer's bedroom.

Lust streaked through him. He walked into the bedroom and looked at the clock. Six-thirty in the morning. By now Archer's detective buddy had probably called him about the latest attack of the Lock Rapist.

He grabbed the remote from the bedside table and turned on the TV. "Come on," he muttered. "Say *something*."

He flipped the channels until he came to a local station that had the words Breaking News on its crawl. He turned up the volume.

"—a break-in and assault early this morning in a subdivision near Vanderbilt University. Authorities are not releasing any information at this time but there is speculation that this could be the latest in the series of vicious attacks and rapes committed by the man known only as the Lock Rapist, named for the lock of hair he leaves at each crime scene. We have with us a professor of psychology at Vanderbilt—"

Earl clicked off the TV, his pulse racing. He was back in the news. It wasn't much but it was better than nothing. "There, Mommy. Now you can see me, wherever you are."

He tossed the coveralls and the jacket into the box in the back of the closet and ran back downstairs. His keys were on the coffee table.

Grabbing them, he rushed out the door and into his car. He had a small window of time to finish scoping out Archer's house and grounds. He never took risks, but he definitely made use of opportunities. And this one was too good to miss, no matter how badly he wanted a shower and some food.

. Until he knew where the weak spots were in Archer's security, he couldn't make his plans to get revenge on Archer and at the same time eliminate the only person who had ever seen him as the Lock Rapist.

He drove toward Archer's house, letting his mind drift back over the past twelve hours and the exquisite satisfaction he felt for a job well done.

RESA SAT in the car beside Archer, her emotions in turmoil. She knew there had been another rape, because she'd overheard the beginning of Archer and Detective Banes's telephone conversation.

The only words Archer had spoken to her were rude, boorish commands.

Get up. Get dressed. You're coming with me.

By the time she'd rushed through her shower and pulled her damp hair into a ponytail, he was dressed and pacing the foyer. He'd hurried her out the door and into his car, not even bothering to tell her where they were going.

She knew that, too, though, because she'd heard him tell Clint he was coming down to the station.

She glanced sideways at his profile. She ought to

be thinking about the latest victim. Or anything other than Archer.

But when she looked at him, all other thoughts flitted right out of her head.

What was it about him? He wasn't traditionally handsome. His features were too rugged, his jaw too strong, his brow ridge too prominent. But his barely contained energy, the intensity of his dark gaze, and his ability to totally focus on whatever was foremost in his mind at the time were all incredibly sexy. Incredibly irritating, but undeniably sexy.

Last night his focus had been centered on her. Right now he was zeroed in on the newest rape. He was obsessed with figuring out what he and everyone else had missed about the rapist and his victims.

Their brief interlude was over. Done. In the past. She knew she shouldn't be disappointed. He'd warned her going in not to have expectations. Not that she needed his warning. She knew if she made too much of it, all she'd end up with was heartache and disappointment.

But she'd found out last night that she wasn't the boss of her feelings. She'd told herself she knew what she was doing. But she hadn't. She'd failed to watch her step and she'd fallen. Hard.

When he'd held her, when he'd kissed her and made love to her, she'd been convinced she was the only thing in his world. She'd felt loved, cherished. For that moment out of time he'd been the center of her universe and she'd thought she had been the center of his.

The sad thing was, she probably had been. For that

one brief moment she'd been the focus of his whole attention.

And all of Archer's attention was an amazing thing. He'd watched her, listened to her, learned everything about her body. He'd coaxed her to heights of erotic pleasure she'd never known existed. He'd made love to every inch of her. He'd made her feel loved, even cherished. And definitely the only person in his world.

Now, though, the moment had passed and, in true Archer fashion, he was focused on the only thing that *really* meant anything to him: catching the man who'd taken his wife away from him.

Resa swallowed against the lump in her throat as he pulled into the police-station parking lot and jumped out of the car. She scrambled after him, catching up to him at the door.

"Stop it, Archer," she snapped. "You can afford the three seconds it takes for me to get out of the car."

He glared at her. "Wait for me in the squad room."

She grabbed his wrist. "Archer, you dragged me down here. The least you can do is let me be involved. I want to see the map. I want to hear the connections. I want to know why he chose my sister and not me. You can't have it both ways. I'm either part of this investigation or I go back home."

She didn't think his dark stare could get any darker. He pushed the door open with more than necessary force.

"Is that a threat? Because believe it or not, I'm not intimidated."

"No. I just—"

"Then if you want to stay here, keep quiet," he growled. "Because if you don't, Clint will kick you out. And if he doesn't, I will."

She nodded and suppressed the childish urge to stick out her tongue at him as he stepped back to let her enter first.

Old wooden desks were crowded together, facing this way and that. Four people were working. They all looked up. Two men raised their hands in a brief wave at Archer. The others went back to their paperwork.

Archer acknowledged the men with a nod as he crossed the room in two long strides and headed down a short hall.

She followed him through a door labeled Interrogation.

Detective Banes was writing on a green chalkboard. Two men in street clothes sat at a scarred table, studying the board and the city map hanging beside it.

"So there's the list of the attacks in chronological order," Banes said, glancing their way as they entered. "And over here on the map are the locations. Each pin represents the scene of an attack."

"You can take my wife's attack out of the equation."

Banes frowned at Archer.

"It's not part of the pattern." He went to the board and picked up the eraser. "Every single attack has taken place in early June or late December, indicating an organization that borders on obsession."

Resa got a glimpse of the notation—Natalie Archer, February, before he wiped it out and tossed the eraser down.

Banes set down the chalk and dusted his hands. His frown was still in place. He wasn't happy that Archer had walked in and taken over.

"What's the deal with June and December?" One of the seated men asked.

"Geoff, this is Detective Ed Thornton. You know Bill Mangum."

"Thornton. You took my position, right?"

"Yes, sir. I'm sorry about—"

Archer waved his hand. "You asked why June and December. That's one of the things we haven't been able to isolate. They're exactly six months apart, but if there's some significance to that, I can't see it."

Resa looked at the dates. "School," she said softly.

Archer's gaze snapped to her. "What?"

"Grade schools, high schools, even colleges let out in late May or early June. And two weeks at Christmas. Maybe he's a teacher."

Archer's eyebrows rose and he nodded. "Or has children himself." He wrote *Teacher?* and under it *Children?* "What else could the dates indicate?"

Thornton's cell phone rang. He answered it and spoke briefly, then stood. "Come on, Mangum. We've got a robbery with injuries."

The two men headed for the door. Thornton turned back. "Detective Archer, it was good to meet you."

Archer nodded.

As soon as the detectives were gone, Banes rounded on him. "What the hell are you doing? If you're thinking about coming back on the job, you can't. You took disability retirement."

Archer's jaw twitched. "Oh yeah, I remember now," he said sarcastically, holding his right hand up like a mock gun. "Can't shoot anymore. Come on, Clint. Call me a consultant or a busybody. I don't care. I need to solve this case."

Banes looked at him for a couple of seconds, then nodded. "You know as much about him as anybody here. Have at it. I've got a meeting downtown in fifteen minutes. I'm already late. I hope they'll agree to give us some help out here. Suit yourself. But don't forget you're unofficial. Don't be ordering my staff around."

"Clint, what about the victim? Do you have her statement yet? Or the physical evidence?"

"Her statement's being transcribed. Basically it's the same story as all the others. No sign of a break-in. Threw a dark cloth over her face, raped her, made her lie down in the bed and tucked the sheets tight around her. Then he left the same way he came in. We probably won't have the analysis of the physical evidence for a couple of days."

"Did she see him?"

Banes sighed. "She's got a little boy, so she has night-lights everywhere, even in her bedroom. She saw his face, but it was pretty dark. We're going to put her with a forensic artist as soon as she's able, but I doubt she has enough for him to go on. She says he didn't have any distinguishing features."

He turned to Resa. "You want some coffee? Let me show you where the break room is. There are magazines. Even a couch you can take a nap on."

She shook her head. "I'll stay here. I want to see all the evidence."

She felt Archer's frown but she ignored him.

"I should be back in about an hour or so." Banes left, leaving Archer and Resa alone. Archer shot her a venom-laced glance, then turned back to the chalkboard.

"Good catch on the dates," he said grudgingly.

She moved closer to the map that was displayed beside the chalkboard. "My mother taught middle school. I remember how her schedule was."

"What about your sister? How's she doing?"

Resa sighed and shrugged. "Mom says she's still not eating, but she has agreed to make an appointment with a therapist." She looked at the positions of pins on the map.

"That's good. Make sure she goes."

She noticed the sad note in his voice. Had his wife refused to go to therapy? If she had, would she have gotten better? Would it have saved her life?

Archer looked at the city map. Then he reached over and pulled out a pin.

Resa saw the muscle in his jaw twitch. "Your house?"

He nodded. "Keeping her attack in the equation just muddies the waters."

Resa looked back at the map. For the first time she noticed the circle drawn with a red permanent marker. Half of the pushpins were inside the circle.

"What's the red circle?"

"Most serial offenders commit their crimes in an area that radiates outward from their home—or sometimes their place of work. They build in what we call a *buffer zone* around their *safe place*—their home or business." He tapped the map. "See this blue circle inside the red one? That's his buffer zone. The theory is that once you've mapped the locations of his crimes, his home will be located within that blue circle."

"How did you know where to put the red circle?"

"We drew the circle around the tightest cluster of the six attacks. But as you see, the rest are scattered. His victims are literally all over the map."

"Are all the attacks in your precinct?"

He stepped closer to her to point. "Nope. See this jagged line? That represents our precinct. But the first two rapes were, so we caught the case."

"So if he were a teacher, these locations would be closer together and his home or school should be somewhere around here." She pointed to the center of the circle.

He stepped over closer to her. "It's never quite that precise, but that's the theory."

She thought about her job. "In my work I have to go *to* my clients. They don't come to me. What if his job takes him to people's homes?"

"Like a plumber or a repairman or a yard man? We

thought of that. But there are literally thousands of people in jobs like that. We still have nothing to go on to narrow the field of possible suspects."

Resa inhaled the faint citrus scent that she would always associate with Archer's dark eyes, his heat and his fierce, gentle lovemaking.

With him this close, she couldn't ignore his magnetism or the tension between them.

Last night he'd been a tender, attentive lover. But this morning it was obvious that he regretted what he'd done. He'd shut down.

Whatever he'd felt in the soft darkness of the night, it had been an aberration, a temporary weakness. She saw the truth in his eyes. He would never let his guard down again.

She went around the other side of the table and sat down. She needed more than a couple of feet of wood between them, but it helped—a little.

"What solid evidence do you have?" she asked.

"Why are you exposing yourself to all this? You're just going to end up upset and feeling more and more helpless and angry about what happened to your sister." He paused. "Trust me."

"Because that monster is after me. I feel frustrated and guilty that he got to my sister when I was supposed to be protecting her. But I won't make that mistake again. I am not like Celia or your other victims. I'm prepared to fight—"

His head jerked slightly, as if he were dodging her words.

His *wife*. "I'm sorry," she exclaimed. "I didn't mean—"

"Forget it," he growled. "I've already told you about the fingerprints. Two partials. One from the bedroom window in my condo and the other from your note."

He turned to the chalk board and wrote *Evidence* then underneath that *Fingerprints*. Then beneath that he wrote *Eyewitness Statement*.

That was her. "For all the good my description was."

"You gave us a good sense of his physical type— white male, around five feet eight inches, wiry build. If this latest victim can give us even a vague description of his features or his hair, maybe we can get one step closer to catching him."

He put down the chalk and massaged his right palm with his left thumb. Then he picked the chalk up again and wrote the attributes as he listed them. "Piercing eyes. Wearing what looked like a dark jumpsuit or coverall, a black hooded jacket and white running shoes."

"What about the physical evidence?"

"The guy is not dumb. He doesn't leave anything behind. He probably—well—leaves his clothes on. We have a couple of unidentified hairs, the pieces of fabric he wraps around their heads and the locks of victims' hair he's left at each scene. But there's nothing to compare them with."

"The fabric? I saw the piece that he'd—covered Celia's face with, but what about the others?"

"They all appear to come from the same length of cloth. Judging by the material, it's probably a curtain he's torn apart. The torn edges fit together. I wouldn't be surprised if we find torn pieces ready and waiting in his car when we catch up to him."

"What about DNA?"

Archer laughed and shook his head. "It's almost impossible for an ordinary town investigating an ordinary crime to get DNA results back."

"An ordinary crime?" Resa's voice cracked on the word *ordinary.*

He nodded grimly. "Sad as it sounds, Nashville and a local crime like this are so far down the priority list... We sent a hair sample found at the second crime scene. It took eleven months to get it back, and we have nothing to check it against."

"But you've profiled him, right?"

"What do you do, watch cop shows all day?"

She lifted her chin. "I watch some. But everybody knows about profiling."

"Not so many know that serial offenders can devolve or escalate. When that happens all bets are off." He propped a hip on the edge of the table and massaged his hand again.

"But, yes, we do have a profile. Our perp is probably in his late thirties or early forties, married with kids. Highly intelligent, almost obsessively organized, which means he most likely holds down a good job. He has the skills to get into the victim's homes without having to break in. Usually through a window. He could be a carpenter, a construction worker or even a window installer." He wiped his face and continued.

"The victims all have several things in common, too. They're blond and slender, and in their mid-to-late twenties. This tells us his choices are not random. But we haven't found anything beyond their looks that's common to all of them."

"Nothing? How can there be nothing?" She heard the anger and disbelief in her voice. A monster had destroyed her sister's life and the lives of the other victims, and he wasn't going to be caught.

Archer leaned across the desk until his face was just inches from hers. "Because this is real life, sweetheart, not a TV show."

Chapter Nine

Archer saw the surprise and hurt on her face. He straightened, feeling like a jerk. "Look—nobody wants this guy more than I do. But TV shows are misleading. Real life cases don't unfold in logical order."

Her mouth tightened and her eyes closed briefly. When she opened them, he could see dampness gleaming in the corners. "I know that." She dropped her gaze to her clasped hands. "I just want this monster. I want him to pay for all the lives he's destroyed."

"Hearing all this is upsetting you. You need to rest. You didn't get much sleep last night." *Ah, hell.* He couldn't open his mouth without sticking his foot in it.

Immediately, his brain clicked through an erotic slide show of images from the night before. He squeezed his eyes shut, trying to cleanse his brain of the evocative pictures. Resa above him. Beneath him. Her hair draped like a silken veil across his flesh. Her mouth, her lips, her sleek, supple body.

"Come on," he growled. "I'm taking you to the

break room. You can get some coffee, maybe lie down. I'll let the guys know you'll be in there."

"No." She sat up straight. "I have to do this. I have to know that I did everything I could."

"You've done a lot. Leave it to the professionals, now."

Resa shook her head. "A lot is not enough. I told you, I won't sit back and let someone else fight my battles. I owe it to Celia. I promised her I'd take care of her."

Archer set his jaw. He looked as if he wanted to take her hand and lead her to the break room like a child. She could imagine him pointing his finger at a chair. *Stay put and try not to get into trouble.*

She met his gaze without wavering.

"The smart thing for you to do—the safe thing—is to let the police do their job. You want the Lock Rapist. So do we all, but it's the police who can get him."

"I don't see you sitting back and letting them do their job."

Archer massaged his palm. "That's different."

"Right." She sat back and crossed her arms and lifted her chin. "How does he choose his victims?"

"The detectives have gathered every bit of information they could find about the victims—where they work, where they buy groceries, their gym, their hairdresser—every place they frequented, and there still aren't enough cross-matches to connect them. We know his victims aren't picked at random. His attacks are too well planned. There's a common thread out there. We just haven't found it yet."

Resa looked at him, considering the few things that did connect all the victims. "Archer, did he leave a lock of hair this time?"

"Sure. Just like every other time." He propped his hip on the edge of the table and flexed his fingers. She was sure he didn't realize that he did it when he was thinking.

"But if he stays true to his profile, this hair would be Celia's, right? My sister?"

"That's right. Where are you going with this?"

"I'm not sure, but can I see it?"

"You want to see the hair sample? Why?"

"Because it's my sister's hair."

He angled his head and considered her. His eyes slid past hers to study her jaw, the angle of her chin, her crossed arms. She felt as if he was measuring her capabilities. Involuntarily she straightened her back even more.

He looked down at his hand. Finally he spoke. "I'll have to check. If the lab techs are finished with it. And if Clint will okay it—then maybe. I don't have the pull I used to have." His mouth turned up in a wry smile, but his voice sounded bitter.

He called Clint, and within a few minutes one of the detectives brought him the evidence bag with a lock of honey-colored hair in it.

"May I see it?" she asked. "I mean, hold it?"

"You can hold the bag. But don't break the seal. I have no authority to reseal it, and you'll break the chain of evidence. Remember, this may be one of the only pieces of evidence we have to connect him to the victims. We can't afford to screw up even one tiny point of evidence." He handed it to her.

Holding the lock of hair the rapist had cut and carried away with him the night he'd attacked her sister made Resa's stomach churn with revulsion.

She took it over to the window behind the chalk-board and opened the blinds. It was Celia's hair. She recognized the shade and the fine texture. Gritting her teeth, she did her best to push away the memory of her sister the way she'd found her that night, curled up in a fetal position, whimpering and shivering.

"Oh, Celia," she whispered. "I should have been there."

She turned the bag over and looked at the hair from the other side. She had no idea what she was looking for. But it had felt vitally important that she see her sister's lock of hair. That she hold it.

She held it a little closer to the window. Her pulse sped up. She squinted and looked at it from different angles, studying each separate strand of hair.

There was no question.

"Archer? There's more than one person's hair in this bag."

"More than one—what are you talking about?"

"Are you sure this sample didn't get mixed up with one of the others?"

"A good cop never excludes any possibility. But that bag was sealed at the scene. And the lab works on one piece of evidence at a time so mix-ups won't happen." He walked over to stand beside her.

She looked up at him. "I'd colored Celia's hair for her just a couple of days before—" She smiled sadly, thinking of her vivacious younger sister. Then the image was replaced by the picture she'd taken away with her from her mother's—Celia staring into space, her hair stringy and unwashed and her eyes dull.

Grief and anger washed over her. She renewed her vow not to rest until the Lock Rapist was brought to justice.

"Resa." Archer's voice intruded gently into her vengeful thoughts. He touched her hand. "You're crumpling the bag. Relax."

He ran a finger along her knuckles, a calming gesture that did anything but calm her. He'd caressed and kissed her knuckles last night. His kisses had started out light and tentative, as if he were as unsure as she about where it was leading.

But his every touch had broken down another layer of inhibition, until she would have been no more able to stop him than she could stop her own breath.

He was still talking and she was still staring at his hand.

"Resa?" He wrapped his fingers around hers and she realized she was trembling. "Calm down. We're going to get him. Now, tell me what you're talking about. What makes you think there are two samples in that bag?"

"I know there are. Look at this."

Instead of taking the bag, Archer moved closer, until his side brushed her shoulder.

She was wrapped in sensation—his hot, hard body, the faint scent of citrus, the calm promise of his low voice. The sensations combined, sending echoes of the night before tingling through her. He bent his head so close to hers that she felt her hair move.

"Show me."

To her dismay, her pulse sped up when his low, gruff voice rumbled in her ear. "Hold it so the sunlight hits it."

She touched his other hand to guide it. Her heart skipped. "Like that."

She clenched her jaw and forced herself to concentrate on the difference between the two locks of hair, rather than the difference between her hand and his larger, stronger one. The fact that they had made love last night was irrelevant. The fact that she wasn't sure she'd ever forget how he felt and smelled and moved had nothing to do with anything.

All she wanted from him was his help in catching the man who'd ruined her sister's life.

She lifted her head and moved slightly away from him. "Do you see the two different strands?"

"No." He turned the bag this way and that.

"Come on, Archer. They're totally different. If you put them under a microscope you'd see it right away. Whoever examined this lock of hair didn't look at the whole sample."

"The tech would have removed maybe ten to twenty hairs. He did put them under a microscope. If there are two different hairs in this bag, he missed it. So show me the different hairs."

"They're all on this side. He cut a thick lock of hair from Celia. All this—" she pointed "—is hers. And these smaller strands right here are not."

"Here?" He slipped his hand from under hers and traced his finger along the plastic bag where the slightly darker strands of hair lay on top of her sister's.

"Yes, that's it."

"I don't see that much difference. That's not just— you know—highlights?"

"Trust me. I know my sister's hair." She took a deep breath and was hit again by his fresh, citrusy scent. Like his nearness, his scent stirred her and brought all the feelings from the night before washing over her. His warm satiny skin against hers. His fierce, tender lovemaking.

Damn it, Resa! She had to stop acting like a love-struck teenager. She was going to be in big trouble if she couldn't forget that lapse in judgment on both their parts.

She cleared her throat. At the same time Archer took a step backward. Had he felt the same yearning as she had? And the same instantaneous regret?

She gave herself a mental shake. *Concentrate.*

"Celia's hair is very fine and she's been coloring it for years. These other strands are totally different. First of all, they're a lot coarser than Celia's. Second, that hair has not been colored. And third, if you even need more evidence, Celia's hair is straight. The un-treated hair is wavy."

She looked up at him. "The rapist left two people's hair at the crime scene."

Archer took the bag from her and looked at it. He was sure she knew what she was talking about. She was a woman, after all, and she obviously knew her sister's hair. But he still couldn't see much difference.

He turned the bag over. He knew those initials—both sets. They belonged to the crime scene investigator and the lab tech. Both of them were men. Both were good at their jobs. Very good. But if a female had processed the scene, if a female lab tech had studied this sample, would they have spotted the differences on sight? Would a woman have been more likely to notice the two different colors that he couldn't see?

"The locks of hair from the first two attacks were analyzed. There were no usable results. We had nothing to compare them to, except each other, and hair from the other victims. Once we discovered that the lock of hair at each rape was from the previous victim, there was no other useful information to be gained."

"How did they check this hair against Celia's?"

"We cut a lock of hair from each victim and bagged it separately." He blew out a frustrated breath. "Now we need to go back and examine the hair that was left at each scene. Maybe he leaves hairs from all his victims, and we missed that."

"These hairs are only from one person. I'd bet on it. And I'll bet every single sample has a few of these." She looked up at him. "They're all going to match."

Archer raised his eyebrows.

"Think about it. There's some reason he takes a lock of hair and leaves one at every single crime scene.

And it's got to have something to do with whoever this different strand belongs to."

"You could be right." He nodded, then rubbed his neck and arched it. "Hold it."

"What is it?"

"What about the first crime scene?"

"He left a lock of hair at his first attack?"

He looked up at her. "Yeah. We figured that it wasn't his first attack. We figured there were other victims out there who hadn't come forward. Hell, he could have attacked women in other cities. That first hair was never identified. Now I'm wondering if that first lock is the same as the few hairs you just found. Those hairs must be from someone important to him. They could be the common thread that connects him to all the victims."

He wanted to compliment her powers of observation, but he wasn't sure how she'd take it. He hadn't been very nice to her today. And then there was that other problem.

He was still reeling from last night and what he'd done. Just standing close to her for those few seconds while she showed him the hair had sent his blood racing. The memory of her supple, graceful body pressed against his had haunted him all morning.

He'd known from the moment he'd first laid eyes on her that she was going to disrupt his life. Then he'd gone and volunteered to protect her. To make it worse, he'd crossed the line. He'd compromised her by giving in to his raging attraction to her. Emotions and hormones screwed with good judgment. What the hell had he been thinking?

"What about DNA?" she asked.

He took two steps backward and shook his head. "The hairs were cut. You can't get a DNA sample unless you have a root. But it's the same problem. We could gather DNA on the victims, but to what end?" His voice was gruff. He cleared his throat. "I'll take this over to the lab, and tell them to check the two different strands."

As he started to turn he caught her gaze. The look in her eyes made him realize what he'd just said. He muttered a curse. "I mean I'll ask one of the detectives if they'll do it."

He knew there was a reason he hadn't spent any time here since his retirement. It was hard as hell to remember that he wasn't in charge, wasn't even a detective anymore. He was nothing but a damn cripple. He flexed his hand then balled it into a fist, quelling the urge to slam it into something.

"Archer?"

He looked up and saw an unwanted compassion in her eyes.

"I'm sorry for what happened to you."

Anger and humiliation crashed down on him like a sudden thunderstorm. That was another reason he'd avoided people all this time. "I don't need your *pity*. You don't know anything about me."

"I know what you told me last night. I know how much you loved your wife. How devastating it was for you to lose your career."

He rounded on her, ignoring the alarm on her face. "Do you know that she wanted me to quit the force? Do you know that if I'd cared about what she wanted, none of this would have happened? She'd still be alive, and your sister might never have been attacked? You want to feel sorry for someone, feel sorry for her and your sister, and the women the Lock Rapist is going to attack in the future because I can't catch him."

Her face drained of color. "I wasn't—I didn't mean—" She clamped her mouth shut and shot him down with her green laser eyes.

"Never mind," she said coldly.

BY THE TIME Archer got back from explaining the situation to one of the detectives and watching him fill out the paperwork necessary to have all the hair samples reexamined, Clint had returned.

Resa was sitting at the table. She didn't look up when he came in. Clint was perched on the edge of the table near her. He stood when Archer opened the door.

Archer frowned at them. "What's going on?"

Resa kept her eyes on her hands.

Clint cleared his throat. "Good news."

Like hell, Archer thought.

"I've been given a couple of people from the Belle Meade precinct. The commissioner is ready to catch the Lock Rapist."

"Yeah?"

"I can free up a position to guard Resa. We'll put her in a hotel with two twelve-hour shifts guarding her."

So that was it. He studied Resa's bowed head, the tense line of her shoulders, her white-knuckled hands. She obviously wanted to be out of there. Why else wouldn't she look him in the eye?

Well, wasn't it what he wanted, too? Didn't he want her out of his house? Out of his life? From the very beginning she'd been a thorn in his side, with that stubborn tilt to her chin and those green eyes.

Maybe if she wasn't there so close to him, he could forget that the night before ever happened. He could go back to his hermit's existence.

"This what you want, Resa?"

She raised her head and reluctantly met his gaze. Her green eyes were wary, as if she didn't know what he might do.

"Well?"

"Isn't it what you want?" she threw back at him.

He glanced at Clint, who was watching them with a bewildered expression on his face. It was no wonder. Tension hung over the room like a rain cloud.

He considered her question. His house would be cavernous and silent without her there. He'd made sure it was that way. It was what he wanted—wasn't it?

She'd dropped her gaze back to her hands, giving him a chance to study her some more. She'd disrupted his existence, given him a reason to care, a reason to live—the last thing he'd wanted.

She'd filled his house and his life with light when

all he'd wanted was darkness. He'd worked out a routine that suited him. He taught a few classes, occasionally saw some of the guys on the job when they came to the range. But when he couldn't take the world anymore, he could have his house all to himself, like a wounded animal slinking off to lick his wounds alone.

An unexpected pang arrowed through the middle of his chest. *Alone.*

He took a deep breath. "I think it's the best thing." He heard the harsh tone in his voice and felt Clint's disapproving gaze.

She nodded, then got up and walked around the table. "So Detective Banes, how soon can I meet my babysitter?"

"Right now." Clint held the door for her. She left without another word.

Archer turned toward the window, but he didn't see the parking lot or the tree-lined streets. All he could see were the photos of the Lock Rapist's victims. And they all had Resa's face.

Chapter Ten

Earl gnawed nervously at a ragged fingernail and looked at the clock on his dashboard. He'd been parked across the street from the police station for over four hours. He'd seen Banes leave and return, but Archer and Theresa were still in there.

Archer's car was parked near the front door of the police station. If he was there, then so was Theresa.

He was happy that so many people were spending so much time on *him*. Detectives, uniformed officers, crime scene investigators, TV reporters. His mom must be so proud. And then there were the women who would have trouble sleeping tonight and every night for a long time.

But he was hungry and tired. His muscles still ached and his head still hurt. And as if that wasn't enough, he had to pee.

He squirmed and tried to find a comfortable position. Damn it, if something didn't happen soon, his bladder was going to force him to abandon his surveillance.

The door to the police station opened. Earl tensed and slid down in his seat. A uniformed officer stood aside and a woman walked past him down the steps to a police car.

What the hell? Earl squinted at her. It was definitely Theresa Wade. He'd half expected the cops to try to fool him with a ringer—a policewoman used as a decoy.

But at least they realized he was too smart to be fooled that way. Earl had watched Theresa enough so that he knew how she walked, how she carried herself.

The thing that surprised him was that she was leaving without Archer following behind her like a pet dog. Where was the cop taking her? He opened the passenger-side door for her, then went around and got in on the driver's side.

As the black and white car pulled away from the curb Earl looked back at the station. What was going on with Archer? There was no way he'd let her go off without him.

Earl cranked his car and put it in gear as the cop car drove past.

After one last glance at the station, Earl pulled out and headed after Theresa. He checked the rearview mirror a couple of times, but by the time he had to turn left to follow the car, Archer still hadn't appeared.

He couldn't believe Archer was letting Theresa leave without him, even if she *was* with a cop. From the moment Archer had realized that Earl had been in her apartment, he hadn't let her out of his sight.

Earl would have bet money that Archer would never trust her safety to anyone else, especially now that there had been another attack. But for some reason, he had.

Earl tailed the cop car. He didn't have time to worry about Archer right now. He couldn't afford to lose track of Theresa.

The cop drove toward downtown and stopped at a high-rise hotel.

A hotel. They were putting her in protective custody. Why now? Archer had taken her home with him to protect her. Now suddenly he was letting her go off without him? It didn't make sense, especially after what Earl had seen last night.

Hey, maybe that was it. Maybe the lovebirds had had a fight. Would that make Archer let her go off with someone else? Earl eased up closer to the cop car.

He might as well quit racking his brain over something he wasn't going to figure out. It didn't matter why Archer had sent Theresa away with an officer—just that he had.

A tingling excitement began to build inside him. Maybe he could get to her, now that she was away from Archer. His muscles began to twitch as they tightened in anticipation.

It was only a matter of time now.

ARCHER RUBBED his wet hair with a towel. The shower hadn't helped much. It felt good to be clean, and the hot water had relaxed him a little. But his gut was still tied up in knots over the latest attack.

He flipped on the bedroom light and froze.

His bed was made. The sheets were smoothed and the bedspread was folded neatly across the foot.

Resa. She'd made his bed. His chest tightened.

Looking at the bed where they'd spent the night, he grimaced. He'd acted like a total jerk after Clint's call this morning, snapping at her to get up and get dressed.

He hadn't had sex in a hell of a long time, but he did remember how to treat a woman, and that wasn't it.

He pushed his fingers through his damp hair as he tried to empty his mind of the memories that floated around him. Her smooth skin, the soft nape of her neck, the taste of her.

His body started to react to his thoughts. He clenched his jaw as he pulled on pajama pants and jerked back the sheet. He lay down and threw an arm over his eyes. But it didn't help. His brain was still in overdrive.

"Relax, damn it," he whispered. "Get her out of your head." Turning over, he grabbed the pillow from the other side of the bed and buried his nose in it— for about a half second.

"Hell!" he muttered, sitting up. He curbed the urge to throw the pillow across the room. Instead, he brought it to his nose again.

His senses went on full alert, just as they had the first time. But this time so did his body. He breathed in the elusive scent that lingered on the pillow. It smelled like melons and sunshine. It was different from anything he'd ever smelled before. It was Resa's scent, and it acted on him like an aphrodisiac. If he didn't do something right away, he was going to have a problem to take care of.

With a groan, he swung his legs over the side of the bed and propped his forearms on his knees. He shook his head. He wasn't about to do anything to sully the memory of last night.

All right, now he was making way too much of it. It was sex. No big deal. She was gone now.

The hell she was. She might be in a hotel downtown, but her unique evocative scent lingered, haunting him. He had a feeling it would never fade from his home, his bed or his head.

He cursed and stood. He reached for the sheets, intending to rip them off the bed and throw them in the hamper with the rest of his dirty laundry.

But he wasn't quite ready to do that.

He turned on his heel and headed out the door, slapping the door facing with his palm. He took the stairs two at a time down to the first floor, then around and down the basement stairs.

He wasn't going to get a lick of sleep anyhow. He might as well do something constructive. Or at least pretend to.

He grabbed his Sig Sauer and a box of cartridges from the locked drawer of his desk and flipped all the lights on as he passed them.

In his lane he ejected the magazine from his gun, ignoring the pain in his hand, and checked it. It was full. He slapped it back into place, then dropped the gun onto the counter.

He rubbed his palm for a few seconds, his fingers feeling the faint ridges marring the back of his hand. He turned his hand over and flexed his fingers. His eyes traced the fine scars that ran like a spider's web from his knuckles to his wrist.

The night before, Resa had traced the scars with her finger, then kissed each one while he confessed to her things he'd never told anyone else—ever. The horror of helplessly watching his wife shoot herself in front of him. The paralyzing fear that he would never regain use of his hand. The crushing disappointment when he realized he had to give up the career he loved.

But he hadn't confessed his worst sin. The thing that kept him from forgiving himself. The thing that kept him obsessed with catching the Lock Rapist.

He rubbed his burning eyes, then picked up the gun. Holding it in his right hand, he pointed it at the target and wrapped his fingers around the barrel. The shortened tendons protested as he fitted his index finger through the trigger guard.

Pain gathered around his wrist, shot up past his knuckles and out through his trigger finger, causing it to tighten reflexively. He winced, waiting for the report.

It didn't happen.

Slightly encouraged, he lifted his arm a little higher, braced his right hand with his left, and squeezed the trigger.

The recoil nearly knocked the gun out of his hand. "Ow, damn it!" He set the gun down and flexed his fingers, working out the cramps. He slapped the recall button.

The target was clean, except for one tiny nick on the lower left edge. A gut-wrenching anguish twisted his insides into knots.

A police officer had to be steady and accurate. A wild shot, a hesitation, could cost a fellow officer or an innocent bystander his life.

He'd been working night and day for months to get his gun hand back. Physical therapy, strengthening exercises, target practice. But nothing was working. There was no way in hell he'd ever be able to handle a gun again.

The last lingering hope that he could one day go back on the job faded. It drained out of him like blood, leaving him empty, defeated. He hadn't realized he'd still harbored so much hope.

He sent the target back downrange, then he braced his hand again. Taking a deep breath and steeling himself against the anticipated pain, he got off four rounds before his hand could no longer hold the gun. It clattered to the counter. He rubbed his hand, grimacing, while sweat dripped down his face like tears.

Then he doubled his left fist and slammed it into the cubicle wall once, twice, again and again and again.

ARCHER WOKE UP to the sound of his cell phone. He sat up, disoriented for a half a second. He was on the couch in his office and his cell phone was on the desk.

He'd finally fallen asleep around four o'clock, after

reading over all the statements of the Lock Rapist's victims. He'd made a list of every single place each one of them had frequented, any repair work they'd had done, any strange events in the weeks prior to their attack.

There were so few things that connected the five women. He'd eliminated his wife's attack. That was motivated by revenge. It didn't fit the pattern.

The police—and he—were missing something. There had to be a vital tidbit of information that the women hadn't thought to mention, or that the detectives had neglected to ask.

The phone rang again. He reached for it, wincing when his overworked hand protested.

"Yeah?"

"Geoff, I think we've got something."

Suddenly he was wide-awake. Something had broken in the case. He could hear the excitement in Clint's voice. His heart leaped. Maybe this was the break they'd been waiting for. "What? What is it?"

"I got the statement from the latest victim. You know we talked about the security system being bypassed?" Geoff paused.

"Yeah?" Archer snapped.

"The company that installed the system is Home Sentry Security."

"Home Sentry? Isn't that—"

"The same company that installed the security system in Resa's old apartment." Clint's excitement crackled through the phone.

"A security company. Damn." Archer's pulse hammered in his temple. "Is it really that simple? I spent last night going over all the victims' statements. None of the other victims mentioned a security system."

"I know." Clint sighed. "I realize it's a long shot, but it's the first real connection—even if it is only between two of the victims. I'm having all the victims reinterviewed. I hate to do it to them, but we need to find out if any of the others have any connection to Home Sentry Security."

"You're planning to interview Resa's sister again? I'm not sure she's up to it."

"Yeah, I know. Since we already know that connection, I won't bother her unless the security angle doesn't work out."

"I want to be there at the interviews."

"I'm not sure that's a good idea, Geoff. The victims are going to be upset enough to have to live through all that again. I'd rather have as few strangers as possible there."

"Where are you going to interview them?"

"I'll probably go to their homes. It'll be less traumatic than bringing them in to the station."

"I agree. Can we at least talk about the questions first? Since we've established that the rapist might have a job that takes him to people's houses to work, we need to cover all the bases. Ask the vics about any home repairs, yard work, anything that might connect them."

"Sure. My first interview is at ten out in Belle Meade. How soon can you get here?"

"I'll be there in less than an hour."

"Good."

"What about Home Sentry Security? Is anyone talking to them?"

"I'm sending Thornton over there this morning to talk to the owner and set up interviews with the employees."

"Great. I want to see what he finds out." He paused. "Clint? Is Resa settled in at the hotel?"

"Childers called me last night. She's fine."

"Tell him to watch her. She doesn't like to be told what to do."

Clint chuckled. "Geoff, if I didn't know better, I'd think you and she—"

"Don't even go there. She's a victim, as much as her sister or any of the others. That's all."

"Sure thing."

"Good."

"Fine."

Archer hung up. So Clint had picked up on the *thing* between Resa and him. He shook his head and brushed a hand through his hair.

Maybe it had been a *thing*, but it no longer was. It was over.

He needed to concentrate on catching the Lock Rapist. He couldn't waste his time and strength on fantasies that would never come to be.

He glanced at the clock. He needed to get dressed and get going. His brain was already cataloguing the questions he wanted to give Clint for the victims to answer.

He gathered up the notes he'd taken the night before and took the stairs two at a time. He had a strong feeling the security company could be the answer. It was the best lead they'd had so far.

"I DON'T CARE what Detective Banes said. I have to do this final fitting. If you won't take me I'll call a cab." Resa stood in the middle of her hotel room surrounded by piles of fabric, her dress form, sewing machine and boxes of beads.

She was just about at the end of her rope. Another officer had brought her sewing supplies to her late yesterday and she'd worked most of the night to finish the fringe on the hem of Chastity's skirt.

Resa had finished and delivered her other designs the week before, thank goodness. Today was her last chance to make any adjustments to Chastity's outfit. It had to fit perfectly, which, with Chastity, was always a problem. If she gained or lost any weight, it could be disastrous for the low-riding skirt or the form-fitting top.

Chastity was leaving the next day on a twenty-city tour. She wouldn't be back in Nashville until the day before the awards. Once Resa did the final fitting, all that was left would be to make any last-minute adjustments to the seams.

The young officer who was babysitting her this morning was clearly at the end of his rope, too. "Ms. Wade, why don't you get your client to come over here? I'm sure she'd understand why you can't leave."

Resa glared at him. "You're suggesting that I just

call up Chastity Sloan and tell her to run over and try on her outfit?"

"Chastity Sloan?" His voice cracked. "Your client is Chastity Sloan?"

Resa smiled to herself. As she'd predicted, the young officer wasn't about to pass up the chance to see Chastity Sloan—and in her own home.

"So do I call a cab?"

"No, ma'am." His face turned bright red. "I'll drive you. I mean, it sounds like it's important."

Resa grabbed up the nearly finished outfit and nodded toward her fittings case. "Get that case and let's go. The appointment's in one hour."

"Yes, ma'am."

That was much too easy. As desperately as she needed to get this last fitting done, Resa wasn't happy about the officer Banes had sent to guard her. Mark Childers was eager, but he was young, inexperienced and impressionable. She didn't feel at all safe, not the way she'd felt with Archer.

She climbed into the police car, wincing in anticipation of Chastity's reaction when Resa drove up with a police escort.

She was so tired of this. The Lock Rapist probably wasn't even seriously after her. Especially now that she was out of Archer's house. As Clint had said, he'd most likely targeted her because of her relationship to Archer.

Maybe he'd leave her alone now that she wasn't anywhere near Archer.

A hollow sense of loss scttlcd dccp in hcr chest. How silly, to miss someone she barely knew.

Barely—ha! That was a lie. She knew him intimately. She'd seen the side of him that no one saw—the vulnerable, heartbroken side. She'd held him as he told her things she knew he'd never told anyone.

And now, she might never see him again.

She stared out the car window, her eyes blurred with tears. How would she live without him, now that she'd known him?

EARL HATED hotels. He never targeted anybody who was staying or working in a hotel. They were too noisy, too busy, and many of them these days had security cameras. They represented risk—too much risk.

But as the old joke went—*why do bank robbers rob banks? Because that's where the money is.*

Theresa Wade was in the hotel, at least for now, so he had no choice.

Still, he was no dummy. All he wanted to do was scare the cops enough that they'd put her back in Archer's house. He already knew what he was going to do to get to her at Archer's. He'd gotten close enough to see Archer's security system. It was a decent one. But for Earl, getting past it would be almost as easy as merely turning a doorknob.

He parked his car a couple of rows over from the police vehicle, in a position where he could watch it, and close to the service entrance at the side of the building.

Just about the time he'd decided he had to take a bathroom break or explode, Theresa and the kid they'd sent to guard her walked out the front entrance and headed for the car. Theresa had a case with her and the cop carried a dress covered by a plastic bag.

Perfect timing.

As the police car drove out of sight, Earl got ready to go in. Just as he opened the car door, his cell phone rang.

A glance at the display told him it was his wife. Muttering a litany of colorful, rude curses, he punched the answer button.

"Hi, honey. Y'all having a good time at your mother's?"

"What do you think? Do you hear the kids in the background? I've had it with them and with Mom. She spoils these kids rotten. We're coming home tomorrow."

Earl's heart jumped straight into his throat, cutting off his air. He gulped and wiped his face. She couldn't come home. Not yet! He racked his brain for a way to keep her at her mother's a few more days.

"Sweetie, I was going to call you tonight. You probably need to stay with your mother a few more days."

"Why? What's going on down there?"

"Nothing. I mean—we, uh, sprung a gas leak early this morning. I called the heating and cooling man. He said there was gas all over the house and he couldn't get to it for a couple of days. You shouldn't bring the kids home until it's all cleaned up and fixed. I'd hate for them to get sick. Or you."

"How in hell did that happen?"

"How should I know? Rusted pipe, I guess."

He heard her sigh. "That's what you get when you buy a cheap house." Her dig rolled off him, just as most of them did these days.

"I guess I can stay up here another day. But you get that thing fixed. I plan to be home by the middle of the week."

"Okay, sweetie. I'll give you a call. I want to be sure the house is aired out before y'all come home. Can't wait to see you and the kids."

"Yeah, right." She hung up.

Earl pressed the off button on his phone and tossed it into the passenger seat. "Oh man—oh man—oh man—oh man—oh man." What was he going to do now?

He had maybe thirty-six hours. He had to make his move tonight or it would be six months before his wife went to her mother's again.

He entered the hotel through the laundry exit and took the service stairs up to the third floor. He found a house phone in the elevator lobby and dialed the front desk.

"Detective Banes here. N.P.D. Connect me with our room please."

The desk clerk hesitated. "Could you repeat that, sir?"

Earl blew out an exaggerated huff. "This is Detective Clint Banes of the Nashville P.D. I need to speak to my officer. He should be registered under Nashville P.D."

"Just a moment, please."

Earl waited nervously. Could the clerk tell that the call had originated from inside the hotel? Was he calling his supervisor?

"Here it is. For your future information sir, the room is registered under a Mr. Mark Childers."

"That's Detective Mark Childers."

"Yes, sir. I'll correct that. Connecting you now."

Earl quickly left his message and hung up, then went out the way he'd come in, through the laundry entrance.

He figured it would be a couple of hours before Resa and the detective returned. He headed home to shower and change clothes. He was going to have a busy night.

Chapter Eleven

Resa stepped into the hotel suite she shared with Detective Childers. She was exhausted. It always drained every last bit of her energy dealing with Chastity, and today was no exception. The young star was high with excitement, getting ready to head out on her twenty-city tour.

For the hundredth time Resa swore she wasn't going to do another outfit for the young diva, but when it came down to it, Chastity paid her top dollar to put up with her temper tantrums and whining. Plus her petite yet voluptuous body was the perfect showcase for Resa's designs. She'd gotten more than one client who wanted to "look like Chastity."

At least now the outfit was done, Chastity was happy with it, and Resa had done everything she could to ensure that the skirt didn't slip down over her hips when she took a breath to sing.

As she set her case down on the floor, she noticed the red light blinking on the phone by the bed.

"There's a message," she said to Detective Childers, who was still glowing from meeting Chastity.

"I'll get it," Childers said, but Resa had already picked up the receiver. She pressed the button and held her breath.

Was it Archer? She knew the chances of his calling her were slim to none, but that didn't stop her heart from pounding and her insides from tingling in anticipation of hearing his low, dark voice.

"Theresa, I'm so glad you feel safe."

Shock coursed through her like electricity and she gasped. She almost dropped the phone.

Childers crossed the room and gestured for her to hand him the receiver, but she couldn't move. The voice held her mesmerized. Her fingers squeezed the plastic receiver until they ached.

The voice droned on. "Enjoy it, because what I did to your sister will be nothing compared to what I'm going to do to you. Get ready. One of us will have a great time. The other one—well, ask your sister and multiply what she tells you by ten, or a hundred. Then wait and wonder. Because one night you'll wake up and I'll be there."

Her legs gave out and she sat down on the bed. She didn't notice when Childers pried the receiver out of her hand. It was several seconds before she realized she was no longer holding it.

He replayed the message, his Adam's apple bobbing as he swallowed. He glanced at her as he listened, his eyes wide with alarm, then ducked his head, hung up and took out his cell phone.

"Archer," she whispered. "Call Archer."

"I have to report it to Detective Banes, ma'am."

Resa put her hand over her mouth. She felt sick to her stomach. The awful words, uttered in that droning, emotionless voice, sent terror sliding down her spine like icy fingers.

She wanted Archer. But Archer didn't want to be bothered with her. He'd seemed relieved that she was being put into protective custody. As if he couldn't wait to get her out of his house.

She'd have liked to think he was doing it for her. That he'd thought she'd be safer this way. But she knew he was confident he could protect her better than anyone.

So why had he let her go?

Detective Childers was talking to Banes, describing the message in detail.

Listening to the words again, and seeing the horror and fear on the young detective's face, Resa felt her stomach rebel. She ran for the bathroom.

By the time she came out, empty and shaking, Childers was waiting with a glass of water.

"Why don't you sit down?"

She shook her head. "We have to get out of here. He knows where we are. Did you call Archer?"

"No, ma'am. Detective Banes is on his way. He wants to talk to you and take a look around before he takes you anywhere. He'll be here in a few minutes."

"But the Lock Rapist. What if he's inside the hotel?"

"He's not, ma'am. Don't worry. He can't get to you in here." He didn't look at all sure he believed his own words.

"You don't know that!" She felt panic pushing up into her throat, straining to erupt into screams. She covered her mouth as if she could stop it.

"Ma'am, please just sit down. As soon as Detective Banes gets here, we'll talk to the hotel staff and find out how they let a call get through to this room."

Resa pulled her cell phone out of her purse and looked at Archer's number. She lifted a shaky thumb to press the quick-dial button, but she couldn't make herself do it. She couldn't bear to be rejected by him again. She'd wait and talk to Clint. Maybe he'd call Archer for her.

She told herself Archer would want to know. After all, he wanted to catch the guy as much as she did. More.

Within ten minutes, Clint was there. He sent Childers to help the other two cops canvass the hotel staff.

"Resa. Are you all right?"

She shook her head. "He found me. How—"

Banes patted her shoulder. "We'll find out. Don't worry. I've already listened to the message from the hotel manager's office and talked to the operator who took the call. He identified himself as me, and the operator bought the lie without checking. Turns out the call originated from a house phone."

"Inside the hotel?"

Clint nodded.

"I knew it. He was here." Resa's stomach turned upside down again. She pressed her fingers against her mouth.

"It's okay. He's not here now. We're taking the digital recorder as evidence. And we're dusting all the house phones for prints. We'll get him, Resa."

"Where's Archer? Did you call him? He'll want to know."

Clint gave her a small smile. "He'll meet us at the station."

She swallowed the tears she could feel gathering in the back of her throat. "You called him. He's coming—" Her voice quit. Relief stung her eyes. He was coming. He'd take care of her.

Banes sat down across from her on the other bed. He leaned forward and took her hands in his.

"Look at me, Resa," he said gently. "Try not to count too much on Geoff, okay?"

His tentative words didn't make any sense. She looked quizzically at him, trying to absorb what he'd said. "Don't count on him—what do you mean?"

He dropped his gaze to her hands. "I just mean— he's been through a lot, and it's affected him. He's not the same man he used to be. I'm not sure if he ever will be. You didn't know him before. He's like a ghost of himself. I'm afraid—"

She held her breath.

"I'm afraid you're going to get hurt."

She shook her head and blinked. A tear fell and

tickled her cheek. "Well, thanks for the advice." A small hiccoughing laugh escaped her lips. "It's a little late, but thanks."

He squeezed her fingers as he sighed. "I had a feeling it was. When you two are in the same room, it feels like some kind of magnetic energy is swirling in the air."

She smiled sadly.

"Take care of yourself, Resa. Protect yourself."

She nodded and pulled away from his grasp. She wiped her eyes just as the door burst open and Archer blew in.

His black eyes zeroed in on her. "Resa, are you okay?" Without waiting for her answer, he confronted Clint.

"Where's the damn message? Here?" He reached toward the phone.

"Geoff!" Banes barked. "Slow down." He stepped between Archer and the phone. "We're taking care of the message and talking to the staff. You shouldn't be here. I told you we'd meet you at the station."

Resa stood. She couldn't take her eyes off Archer. Clint's words echoed in her ears. *Don't count on him.* But she did. She was counting on him for so much.

He sent Clint a cutting glare, then went straight to her. "Are you sure you're all right?"

She tried to nod.

"Don't lie to me, Resa. Look at you. You're pale as a ghost. What did the bastard say?"

"Geoff. I'll let you hear the recording as soon as we get Resa to safety."

"Safety? Are you kidding me?" Archer slipped his arm around her and pulled her close to his side. "She's not going anywhere except with me."

"Geoff—"

"Nope. That's the end of it. I'm not letting her out of my sight again."

"Resa," Banes appealed to her. "This is not a good idea. We need to get you out of town. I'd like to have one of my officers take you to your mother's until all this is over."

Archer's arm tightened. "She's staying here. *I'll* keep her safe."

She heard the censure in his voice and winced. Clint had done everything he could to protect her. Archer was being unfair.

She ought to be relieved that he was taking her home with him, where she knew that anyone who wanted to get to her would have to go through him. But Clint's warning echoed in her ears and combined with her own fears.

Archer was obsessed with the Lock Rapist. As much as she wanted to believe his primary concern was for her safety, she couldn't shake the feeling that he wanted her with him because she was his key to catching the killer.

RESA WAS nearly paralyzed with exhaustion by the time she and Archer left the station at midnight. He guided her to the passenger side of his car and helped her fasten her seat belt. Then he got into the driver's side and turned the key.

The next thing Resa knew he was standing at the open passenger door, reaching across her.

"Archer," she murmured sleepily, drawing in a deep breath of warm, rain-heavy air mixed with his unique citrusy scent.

"Just unhooking your seat belt. Come on. Are you awake?" He straightened and stepped back. "Need help getting out?"

She yawned, then squeezed her eyes shut. "No, I'm fine." She made an effort to open them, but it was too hard. "I'm just a little tired."

"Yeah." His gruff voice rumbled through her as he bent down and cupped her face in his palm. "Resa, come on. Wake up."

She tried. She really tried.

"Okay, Sleeping Beauty. You asked for it."

Before her tired brain could process what he'd said, he kissed her. Thoroughly.

The sensation of his lips on hers, his tongue playing with hers, streaked through her, banishing every last wisp of drowsiness. Suddenly she was awake and hyperaware—of his mouth, his breath, his hand caressing the nape of her neck and the tender underside of her chin.

Just as sharp, just as clear, was her response. Her drowsiness floated away. She reached up, sliding her fingertips along his stubbled jaw and around to touch his lips.

Then he was gone. She sat up. Where had he—

She blinked. There he was, leaning against the open passenger door, his arms crossed and a curious smile curving his lips. "Awake now?"

She frowned up at him. Was he *smirking* at her? She recognized that smile. It was the Cheshire Cat's satisfied grin.

Muttering a couple of rude words, Resa got out of the car. She suppressed a groan when her tired limbs protested.

Archer held out his hand but she ignored it and stepped around him. By the time she got up the steps to the front door, he'd locked the car and vaulted up behind her. Reaching around her, he unlocked the door and opened it, then stepped back.

As she went inside, she realized all she had was her purse. "My bags are still—"

He held up her small suitcase. "I'll get the rest out of the car tomorrow. Tonight you're going upstairs and straight to bed."

"But I want to find out about the phone message and the newest victim and—"

Archer held a finger to his lips. "Shh. You won't remember anything tonight. After all, you were sitting right there the whole time we were discussing it at the station. How much of that do you remember?"

"I—" She remembered being there, but that was all.

"See? Now go to bed, and I promise we'll talk about the evidence tomorrow."

"Tomorrow."

A minuscule chuckle escaped Archer's lips. "Your eyes are crossing. Go on."

"Aren't you coming—" She stopped when his dark eyes snapped to hers.

She felt her face burn. "I didn't mean—"

All she'd meant was that she didn't want to be left alone. She wanted him there while she slept. He didn't have to touch her—didn't have to do anything. She just needed to know he was there.

"I'll be down in the range for a while." The gruffness was back in his voice. "You remember how to reach me if you need me? Hit the Intercom button on the phone or press two on your cell phone. That's the quick code for my cell."

If she needed him. She nodded and took her bag from him. She yawned again. "Sorry I fell asleep on you."

"You're exhausted. Get a good night's sleep."

"You'll be here?"

"All night. I promise you I won't go anywhere without you. And you sure as hell aren't going anywhere without me. Not again."

She felt as though she were floating on air. If only he meant those words the way she wanted him to.

"Archer—thanks."

RESA TURNED OVER, searching for a cool spot on the pillow. A low rumble filled the air—the unmistakable sound of rain. She opened one eye a little bit. Still dark.

She sighed and tried to go back to sleep, but her brain was wide awake. Sighing, she peered at the bedside clock. Ten o'clock? That couldn't be right. It had been after midnight when she got into bed—hadn't it?

Oh no! It wasn't ten at night. It was ten in the morning. The room was dark because of the rain. Why hadn't Archer woken her?

She got up and showered quickly, then dressed in a sundress and sandals. She shouldn't have slept so late. She was anxious to hear what Clint had found out about the voice message the Lock Rapist had left. She shivered, thinking about that creepy voice.

In the hall, she glanced into Archer's room. The bed looked too neat. A sliver of panic lodged in her breast.

He hadn't come upstairs. He hadn't slept in his bed.

He's here, she reassured herself, pressing a hand to her throat. He'd promised.

She flew down the stairs and through to the kitchen. The coffeepot was on. That made her feel better. She poured a cup, grimacing at the slightly burned flavor. He must have made it hours ago.

Cup in hand, she hurried to the front of the house and down to the basement.

He had a hip propped on the edge of his desk, and was massaging his right palm. He looked as if he hadn't slept a wink. His hair was tousled, his jaw stubbled and his eyes red.

He looked up at her and her heart flipped over. How

could he look so awful and so beautiful at the same time?

"You didn't come up to bed last night." As soon as the words were out, she realized how they sounded. "I mean—you spent all night down here shooting, didn't you? Not even you can get along with no sleep."

It was a good thing Resa's question was rhetorical, because Archer didn't think he could speak. She'd appeared in the doorway of his office looking like an angel. The pale-green dress swirled around her slender shapely legs and left her arms bare. He didn't think he'd ever seen anything as sexy as the gentle curve of her shoulders or as beautiful as her freshly washed face.

He was fighting not to acknowledge where his brain had taken him at her careless words.

Come to bed. It was going to be hard as hell being around her, now that they'd made love. It was torturous knowing how her skin smelled and tasted, remembering the almost painful ecstasy of her tightening around him as he pushed her relentlessly toward climax.

Argh. He clenched his jaw and cleared his throat. "Have you eaten?"

She shook her head. "You should have woken me. Have you heard from Clint this morning?"

"I was going to call him later." He glanced at his wall clock. "Hell, it's almost ten-thirty."

He rubbed his burning eyes and stood. "Come on, I'll fix some breakfast, then I'll call and see what he's got."

Resa shook her head. Her soft hair moved and shimmered like iridescent silk. "I'll fix breakfast. You call Clint."

Upstairs, Archer left Resa in the kitchen and walked out onto the back porch as he dialed Clint's number. She sent him an irritated glare, but she didn't comment.

Clint's voice was almost drowned out by the sound of the rain. "Clint, what have you got for us?" He breathed deeply. The smell of freshly turned earth floated on the raindrops. He stepped back from the edge of the porch, looking for a place where the sound of rain on the tin roof was muted.

"I figured I'd hear from you hours ago," his friend said dryly. "You sleep late?"

"The phone works both ways."

"Yeah, well. I've been busy."

"Good. What have you found out?"

As Clint quickly went over the physical evidence from the latest crime scene, Archer caught a whiff of fresh coffee and something that smelled delicious. His stomach growled. He couldn't even remember the last time he'd eaten.

He started to go back inside when Clint's words stopped him in his tracks.

"He took a gun from the victim's bedside table."

Archer cursed. "Why are we just finding this out?"

Clint sighed. "Our victim just remembered. And before you say it—yeah. The drawer where she kept it was unlocked. Her kid could have gotten his hands on it at any time."

"Now he's got a gun," Archer said. "What the hell is he going to do next?"

"That's what we've got to figure out."

Archer wiped a hand over his face and then sent it around to rub the back of this neck. He stepped into the kitchen just as Resa put two plates of French toast on the table.

"What did we find out from the hotel?" he asked.

"I'm waiting for a report on the prints from the house phone. I've got an officer interviewing all the staff. Someone had to have seen him. Meanwhile, I'm reinterviewing the previous victims, starting in about ten minutes. I'll get with you later."

"Ask them whether they've ever talked to a security company or ever gotten an estimate."

"Believe it or not I'd already thought of that one. Keep Resa inside. I'll talk to you later."

Archer pocketed his cell phone and poured himself a cup of coffee. By the time he sat, Resa was already seated across from him and waiting expectantly.

"Archer—"

He nodded as he dug into the French toast. "This is good," he said, gesturing with his fork.

She made an exasperated sound. "I'm glad you like it. Would you *please* tell me what Clint said?" Her fingers were white-knuckled around her cup.

"He's reinterviewing all the victims, trying to establish a connection through a home security company. We won't hear anything from the hotel for a few hours yet." He paused. "There's something else."

"Something else?"

"The Lock Rapist took a gun from the home of the latest victim."

She dropped her fork. It clattered against the china plate.

"A—gun?"

He looked at her steadily, wishing he could change the truth, feeling helpless.

Resa compressed her lips and nodded. "So he's still out there. Nobody can figure out who he is or where he is. And now he's got a gun. So what now?"

"Resa, there's no way he can get to you. I swear I'm not going to let you out of my sight again."

She gave him an odd look and pushed her chair away from the table. She rose, walked over to the kitchen window and stood with her back to him. "He's been out there for three years and you're no closer to catching him than you were the first day." Her voice quivered as if she were holding back tears. "What am I supposed to do, stay here forever?"

Her words sucker-punched him. The idea of her always being here, of his seeing her every day in his kitchen, going to her every night in his bed, sent his emotions into a dizzying tailspin and pushed all thoughts of the Lock Rapist out of his head.

He thought he'd accepted that the rest of his life would be lonely. He'd even reveled in his isolation—for a while.

But then she'd come along and thoroughly disrupted his solitary existence. And now, when he looked at a future without her, it filled him with dread and a hollow emptiness that felt like an abyss.

He went to her, standing so close it was torture not to reach out and pull her against him. Just the thought of holding her stirred his body into arousal.

"I can't promise you much," he whispered, clenching his fists to keep from wrapping his arms around her.

She turned and looked up at him. The trust in her eyes terrified him. But there was something else there that frightened him even more. Something he knew he could name if he had the courage. But he didn't.

"I don't need much," she murmured.

He took a step backward. His gaze traveled over her face looking for what—he wasn't sure. Maybe proof that he'd been mistaken about what he'd thought he'd seen in the green depths of her eyes.

"What I can promise you is that I will protect you with my life. No one will hurt you as long as I'm alive. Do you believe me?"

She nodded and gave him a little smile, but it didn't reach her eyes. She averted her gaze slightly, looking somewhere over his shoulder. "Of course I do," she said. "Thank you."

"I'm going to take a shower. You stay inside. Don't do anything. Don't answer the phone. Don't even look out the window. I'll be done inside of ten minutes. Haven't you got some sewing or something you could be doing?"

"I'll clean up the kitchen, then come upstairs. I

have a couple of hours of beadwork I need to do on an evening dress."

"Good." He stood there for another few seconds, wanting to reach out, to hold her. To be held by her. But he was so damn scared.

Scared he'd love her and she'd die. Scared he'd fail her the way he'd failed his wife. Scared that she was just fascinated with him because he knew what she'd been through.

She raised her chin and took a deep breath, but before she could say anything, he turned on his heel and walked away.

Chapter Twelve

Earl Slattery's armpits and back stung with sweat. He wiped his face and stared at the answering machine, the ominous words ringing in his ears.

This couldn't be happening. Not now. He was running out of time as it was. With a finger that shook he pressed the play button again.

"Hey Earl, it's Dave. Where are you? You'd better be sick and not playing hooky from work. Got some weird news for you. I just got through talking to a damn police detective. He's questioning everybody about some woman being attacked. You and Bronson were the only ones not here today. So I gave him your names. You'll probably be hearing from him."

"Oh man—oh man—oh man—oh man—oh man." The sweat ran cold and clammy down his torso. He paced back and forth across his small living room, trying to think. Trying to plan.

He doubled his fists and pounded his temples.

Dave's words kept repeating in his head. He couldn't stop his brain from racing too fast to make sense. He squeezed his head between his hands.

Why was everything suddenly falling apart? He'd been so careful. "I've never taken risks, Mom. It's always worked before. Why's everything going wrong now?"

His wife and kids would be back tomorrow. The police were closing in. And Theresa Wade was still out there under Archer's protection.

Well, not for long. Earl rushed into the kitchen and pulled his coverall and hooded jacket out of the clothes dryer.

It was down to the wire. He had to take care of her tonight.

He shook out the coverall and rolled it up, then rolled the jacket around it. He stuffed them inside the duffel bag along with his gloves and the small set of tools that got him past any locks or security systems.

Then he took the bag upstairs. He knelt down and pulled the box out of the back of his closet. He lifted the lid.

There it was. The closet light reflected blue off the little .22. It wasn't much of a gun, but when he'd spotted it on his latest victim's bedside table, he'd grabbed it. Now he was glad he had.

He knew how to use it, thanks to the couple of years he'd worked as a night guard before he'd gotten married. He stuck the gun in the duffel bag and set it on the landing.

He looked at his watch. It was hours until dark. Hours to wait, wondering when the police were going to show up to question him about his whereabouts.

He didn't have an alibi, but that was probably better than a false one. He didn't like to depend on other people. Too much risk. He was better off claiming he was home alone. That was much harder for the cops to disprove.

Earl wiped his clammy hands down the front of his pants. He went across the hall to the kids' bedroom. The bunk beds and the trundle underneath were unmade.

He straightened the sheet on the top bunk and tucked it in.

Earl, Junior. *His oldest son.* He adored him. He loved all three of his children—more than anything. They proved he was capable of good—didn't they?

What was he going to do after tonight?

He walked around the small room, touching a baseball, securing a loose pushpin in a pop-star poster, picking up a pair of sneakers and setting them inside the closet. Finally he sat down on the bottom bunk and buried his face in his hands, his whole body quivering.

After tonight he'd no longer have a family. He'd have to disappear—get as far away from Nashville as he could. There was no way he would allow his compulsion to taint his children's young lives. He'd never see them again. But they'd be better off without him. They'd have their mother.

He'd had to grow up without his mother. That's why he'd always worked so hard to protect theirs.

He couldn't stop, couldn't change what he was. The inferno that grew inside him was too greedy. It would never let him alone.

But he could assure that his children had their mother. He longed to curl up into a fetal position on his youngest's narrow bed. But he had to go. The police could be here at any second.

He touched each pillow one last time, then grabbed his duffel bag and rushed out to his car.

THE BLUE FLASH of light nearly blinded him. He cried out and dived forward as the gun's report echoed in his ears. Twenty-five yards downrange, the target swayed as the bullet struck it. Then, slowly, it crawled forward on the pulley. As it got closer, he realized the silhouette had a face—a pretty oval face with wide green eyes and brown hair that shimmered in the harsh firing-range lights. Then he saw the hole. It was tiny, hardly visible. And it was right in the middle of her chest.

He reached out to cover the hole with his hand, to mend it. Then another gunshot split the air.

Archer vaulted out of bed, reaching for his weapon before he was totally awake. His pulse hammered in his throat as he shook off the haze of sleep and got his bearings.

The silhouette with Resa's face had been a dream. But the gunshots—they were real. He stepped into his jeans and tugged them up over his buttocks and fastened them, then slid his feet into loafers.

He eased open the door to the hall about the same time as Resa's door opened. She peered out, her face pale and her eyes wide and frightened.

"Were those gunshots?" she whispered.

"Get back inside. Have you got your weapon?"

She nodded apprehensively. "In my purse."

"Get it and wait there. Lock the door. Don't turn on any lights and stay away from the window. I'll be right back."

"Can I—"

"No!" He waited until she closed the door and he heard the latch turn, then he slipped down the stairs and into the kitchen, avoiding the window over the sink. He'd had the impression the two shots had come from the back of the house, from the area of the outdoor shooting range.

But now everything was silent. Too silent.

He sidled along the far wall to the back door and looked out through the glass. Dark, wispy clouds drifted across the moon, playing hide and seek with the shadows on the ground.

The cast-iron targets scattered over the firing range appeared to dance like stiff-necked ghosts in the wavering moonlight. The berms banking the sides and back of the range sucked up the light like black holes.

Archer watched for a few moments, but nothing moved except the shadows. His pulse returned to normal and his neck and shoulders relaxed a bit. Those shots had sounded close, but maybe it was just his neighbor shooing away stray dogs.

He sucked in his breath and slid his SIG into the waistband of his jeans and turned to head back upstairs.

A shot rang out, followed immediately by the clang of metal.

Archer whirled and whipped out his gun. That was one of his targets.

"Son of a—" he muttered as he searched the range with his gaze. He still didn't see anything. Rather than go out the kitchen door and display himself like a sitting duck against the whitewashed porch, he double-checked the dead bolt and the chain on the door, then backed out of the kitchen into the living room.

He exited silently through the front door and turned on the alarm. Resa wouldn't trip it unless for some reason she came downstairs and tried to open the outside doors.

He circled around the hidden side of the house, moving in its shadow. As he circled around shrubs and avoided twigs and brush, he squeezed the handle of his gun with his left hand and fingered the trigger, trying to convince himself it felt right and comfortable.

At the far corner of the house he stopped. Another few feet and he'd be able to see the outdoor firing range stretching into the field. Of course, by the time he was able to see the range, whoever was out there would be able to see him.

Crouching over, he moved as quickly as he could to the near edge of the back porch, keeping the pillars between himself and the range.

He had a sinking feeling he knew who it was. Those shots weren't accidents. They were deliberate. In fact, they were damned cocky, especially the one aimed at the target. Whoever was out there was trying to draw him out.

Flattened against one of the porch pillars, he patted his pockets. *Damn.* He didn't have his cell phone.

He looked upward, toward Resa's bedroom. "Call Clint, Resa. Dial 911," he mouthed silently.

She was smart. When he didn't come back within a few minutes, she'd call the police.

Suddenly another shot rang out. The bullet zinged off the pillar near his head. He ducked, then angled out and got off a quick shot.

His shot went wild. He knew it as soon as he squeezed the trigger. He shifted the SIG to his right hand, but those already tense muscles spasmed when he tried to grip the handle. He switched it back to his left, cursing silently. What kind of damn protector was he if he couldn't even shoot a blasted gun?

He heard Resa's voice in his head, as if she was standing next to him. *Come on, Archer. How long are you going to bury yourself in that basement, wallowing in your own pity?*

"It stops now." As near as he could tell, the shot aimed at him had come from the other side of the lean-to that marked the firing line.

He peered around the edge of the pillar until he could see the lean-to, but nothing was moving. Taking a deep breath, he dived onto the painted wooden floor of the porch. He crawled across the floor, staying behind the pillars as much as he could, until he got to the far side of the house. He didn't hear anything. So far so good.

Then a twig snapped. He leaned his back against the last pillar and pushed himself upright. Then he angled around, leading with his weapon, prepared to fire. He saw movement—a dark shape darting across the open area downrange, about twenty yards away from the edge of the porch.

The shadow wound through the targets. The black slabs of iron had been cut into the shapes of predators—both human and animal. If the shadow were to stop dead-still, Archer would have a hard time picking him out among the other shapes.

He kept the man in his sights as he braced his left hand and carefully began to squeeze the trigger.

A cloud covered the moon. Suddenly the whole range was cloaked in darkness. It left him at a disadvantage for more than one reason.

Each time he moved or raised his head, he was silhouetted against the white house, whereas the shooter was backed by darkness, even in the open, unless the moon's light happened to hit him just right.

Archer heard the shooter moving closer. Just to keep the guy from closing in, he fired off three shots blindly. His volley stopped the other man's advance for a moment, but then Archer heard his stealthy footsteps again, coming closer to the house.

He darted from one pillar to another, back to the other side of the porch, away from the range. He slid off the edge to the ground as quietly as he could and headed around the house toward the front.

If he were very lucky and very quiet, he could get the shooter between him and the house. Then *he* would have the advantage.

Trying to move without a sound, and straining to hear any move the shooter made, Archer circled the front of the house and came up on the north side, hiding behind the old pickup he kept to drive around his place.

He crouched, listening.

Nothing.

Cautiously he raised his head, his left hand braced in his right, aiming the gun at the pillars that lined the back porch. He couldn't see anything. The moon was still obscured by clouds.

He didn't want to take a blind shot now. It would give away his position.

Then the moon appeared and Archer got a glimpse of the shooter—much closer than he'd anticipated.

He fired, and saw a puff of white where he hit the corner of a pillar. He squinted and aimed again, steadying his hand against the cool metal of the truck's hood. The shooter stepped out from behind the pillar.

Archer squeezed the trigger. But as soon as he did, something slammed into his hand and his gun went flying into the air. A fraction of a second later, he heard the gunshot, then the thud as his weapon landed somewhere behind him.

He whirled and dived toward the sound.

Running footsteps crunched across gravel.

He crawled rapidly, feeling around him, searching for his weapon.

Then the footsteps stopped. A loud crack echoed in his ears and a sharp pain pierced his temple.

Suddenly blood was in his eyes, his left hand was useless, and his body felt like lead.

A buzzing sound filled his ears.

"Resa—" he muttered. Then everything went black.

EARL WATCHED Archer's crumpled form from a few yards away. The detective had cried out twice, but now he lay unmoving on the ground. Earl had seen his left hand jerk, seen his weapon fly in a tumbling arc behind him.

It had been a great shot—a world-class shot. Earl's chest swelled with pride. He'd outgunned a policeman.

He looked with fiendish satisfaction at the blood streaming down Archer's face.

Two world-class shots. He'd grazed Archer's temple with his second shot. He'd crippled the arrogant detective. Now let him try to catch the Lock Rapist.

Part of him wanted to finish Archer off, to stand

above him and put a bullet point-blank into his head. But he had a better plan than killing him. He was going to enjoy every second of this.

But meanwhile, the inferno within him was flaming. He glanced toward the house. He had to find Theresa Wade.

He spotted the sensors on the back door immediately. It was a decent security system. Nothing top of the line, though. Obviously Archer thought he didn't need help keeping his home safe.

Earl ran around to the front of the house, retrieved his wire snips from his tool kit and disabled the alarm on the front door in twelve seconds flat. It took only a few seconds longer to pick the dead bolt.

As he entered the house silently, giggles bubbled up from his chest at the thought of dragging Theresa out into the yard. He'd wait for the moon to come out from behind the clouds, then he'd force Archer to watch.

He shut the front door behind him and locked it. If Archer managed to get up, even if he managed to find his gun in the darkness, he'd have a hell of a time unlocking the door with two useless hands.

Earl stepped into the foyer. He took note of the stairs leading to the basement firing range, then turned to the opposite door.

After a brief examination to be sure there wasn't a second security system guarding Archer's living quarters, he picked that lock and stepped inside.

There to his left were the stairs to the second floor,

where Theresa's bedroom was. He licked his lips as he imagined her cowering in her room, door locked, waiting for Archer to rescue her.

Earl looked at his watch, feeling the time pressure. He had to hurry. He'd fired the first shot eleven minutes ago. Archer hadn't called the cops before coming downstairs to investigate the noise. He wasn't the type. He'd check things out himself first.

Even if he or Theresa had called after he came outside, Earl probably still had about nine minutes before sirens announced the police's arrival.

Plenty of time.

RESA STOOD at the top of the stairs, her weapon clutched in her hands. She'd heard something. Just a slight rattling. It could have been caused by the wind, or the house settling. But she didn't think so.

Archer had been gone too long. And she'd heard more gunshots—a lot more. Each crack had torn through her as if they'd been aimed at her.

As soon as the shots had started, she'd called 911, but she had no sense of how long ago that was. She only knew that the gunshots had stopped.

Her heart banged against her chest wall. The silence was more ominous than the gunshots had been.

What if Archer were wounded, or—

Somewhere below her a board creaked. Resa stifled a scream. Her hand tensed around her little Glock. It wasn't Archer. He'd already be up the stairs calling for her.

It had to be the Lock Rapist. He was in the house.

Panic closed her throat. *Archer.* Where was he? He'd promised she'd be safe as long as he was alive. But the Lock Rapist was here, and Archer wasn't.

Oh, please, God, don't let him be dead. Her pulse pounded so loudly in her ears that it was all she could hear. She glanced toward her room, toward Archer's room, her thoughts swirling like a tornado.

She could hide in one of the bathrooms, or use a bed as a bunker. But what if she hid and waited until he had her cornered—and then she couldn't take the shot? She'd gotten pretty good with the targets, but facing a real person was a totally different story.

Could she shoot someone if it meant her life? Could she face the man who'd ruined the lives of the two people who meant more to her than anything else in the world, and kill him?

She didn't know, but if it came to it, she'd have to try. Right now she needed to get downstairs and check on Archer.

But she'd never be able to get past the Lock Rapist. And the only way she could do that was to sneak past him. She could hide in the linen closet opposite the head of the stairs. If he came upstairs, he'd head for the bedrooms, wouldn't he?

Once he went into one of the rooms, she could run downstairs and out of the house. Surely the police would be there by then.

She slipped into the closet, leaving the door cracked slightly, and gripped the Glock the way Archer had taught her. She waited, hyperaware of each small sound. She heard nothing except her own labored breathing.

She concentrated on breathing evenly, silently, but she didn't have that much control.

She heard the stairs creak again, and then the heavy footsteps came closer. Stiff with apprehension, Resa waited.

Then the sound of the footsteps changed. The Lock Rapist was there—on the second floor. Only the wooden closet door separated them.

Holding her breath, she waited for him to walk away from the closet toward a bedroom. But he didn't.

Silence enveloped her.

"Come on out, Theresa."

The calm words sliced through her like a chef's knife. She jerked. Blood pumped through her head, her limbs, every inch of her body. It felt like boiling water in her veins. She didn't—couldn't move.

The door swung open and there he was. The Lock Rapist. He looked...normal. For some reason that frightened her more than anything else she knew about him.

She gripped her weapon in hands that were numb with fear.

"I promised you, didn't I, Theresa? I told you one of us would have fun. Tell me, are you having fun yet?"

She couldn't speak.

"It's time for you to drop the gun."

"Where's Archer?" She sounded like a frightened child.

An odd, high-pitched laugh answered her. "Don't look for him to come rushing to your rescue. He can't."

No, please. "What did you do to him?"

"You're wasting my time, Theresa. Come out of the closet. Or I'll drag you out."

Despite his ominous words, suddenly the blood-boiling terror drained out of her, leaving her feeling eerily calm.

She was done panicking. A cold anger settled deep in her chest. She might be cornered. She might be doomed. But she didn't have to go without a fight. She'd use every last grain of strength in her body to get to Archer. She had to know if he was all right. She had to see him one more time.

Tightening her finger on the trigger, she shook her head. "Just try," she growled.

The man aimed his gun at her feet and shot.

Resa shrieked and dropped her gun. Before she could even register that she hadn't been shot, the Lock Rapist grabbed her arm and yanked her out of the closet. She fell hard onto her knees.

Her gun was a few feet away. She lunged for it but the man kicked her in the ribs, sending her sprawling. Then his heavy boot pinned her wrist to the floor and a gloved hand grabbed the gun.

"Get up!"

His boot was crushing her hand. She couldn't move. All she could do was gasp for breath. "Go to hell."

He removed his foot and pushed the cold circle of his gun barrel into the back of her neck. "Get up, you meddling whore." She tried to push herself up, but her arms and legs wouldn't support her.

"I can't." Her voice was raspy. Her chest was so tight she couldn't breathe. She cringed against the expectation of a bullet slamming into her flesh. "Go ahead, shoot me."

"Oh no, sweetheart. You're not going that quickly, or that easily."

Then the gun's barrel was gone from her neck. Resa sucked in a breath and tried to make her legs work.

But immediately, a leather-gloved hand fisted in her hair and her attacker jerked her head up. "We're going outside, so your lover Archer can watch."

She heard his words through the pain that brought tears to her eyes. But if he ripped every hair out of her head it didn't matter.

Archer was alive.

"You've got your choice. You can walk down the stairs or I can drag you." His fist grew tighter.

She whimpered.

"Okay. I'll drag you. That'll be fun."

"I can walk," she gasped.

"What did you say?" He jerked her head up again and put his face in front of hers.

The face of the Lock Rapist. This was the man who'd ruined so many women's lives. This pasty-faced, puny little man with his close-set dark eyes.

She knew those eyes. She'd seen him that night.

She wanted to spit in his saggy, puffy face, but she couldn't gather enough saliva to swallow, much less spit.

"I'll walk," she croaked. She gathered all her will and pushed herself to her knees, then, with the help of his jerking on her hair, she managed to get to her feet.

He kept his fist in her hair and put his other arm around her, shoving the barrel of the gun into the soft flesh under her chin.

"Let's go."

He pushed her forward. She grabbed on to his forearm to keep from falling. Between his shoving and her desperate effort not to fall, they made it down the stairs and through the house to the back door.

He shoved her hard up against it and pressed his body obscenely against hers.

"Unlock the door and take off the chain."

Resa let go of his surprisingly strong arm and fumbled for the lock.

"Stop stalling! I told you Archer can't save you. He couldn't even save himself."

She finally turned the latch and slid the chain off. By now her eyes were streaming tears. Where was Archer? If he weren't hurt, the Lock Rapist would have never gotten in the house. "What have you done to him?"

"I told you to shut up." He jerked open the door and shoved her through it. She fell to her knees and tried to scramble away, heading across the porch toward the concrete steps. But he was too fast. He had her hair again.

She saw a flash of movement, and then pain exploded in her temple. "Try anything else and I'll knock you out."

Her temple throbbed, and she felt a warm stickiness running down her cheek. He must have conked her on the head with the gun's barrel.

"What's—" she gasped. "What's your name?"

He pushed her down the steps. Only his grip on her hair kept her from tripping.

"Me? I'm the Lock Rapist," he said. "Don't you *recognize* me?"

There was a note of pride overlaying the anger. He pulled her head back and stuck his face in front of hers again. "Remember? You saw me that night. How's your sister doing?"

She curled her fingers and scratched at his face. She connected with the side of his neck and felt flesh rip and sticky blood coat her nails.

"Ow!" He grabbed her wrist and twisted it until the bones rubbed together. She bit her lip to keep from crying out as she waited to hear her bones snap.

"I'm getting tired of you, Theresa. Now if you don't quit wasting time, I'll have to really hurt you." He let go of her arm and dragged her by her hair toward the pickup.

She grabbed his leg, trying to trip him, but all her efforts didn't even slow him down. He just kicked at her as if she were a bothersome terrier.

She kept trying, though. Finally a broken fingernail snagged in the material of his pants and she caught a handful of cloth. She jerked and he tripped and fell to his knees, losing his grip on her hair.

She dived toward his gun hand. She managed to stretch far enough to touch the tip of the barrel before he kicked her. His boot caught her under the chin. The blow stunned her for a few seconds.

"You're just a barrel of fun, aren't you, Theresa? Much better than your sister."

All she did was lie there.

His breathing was labored as he scrambled to his feet and grabbed her hair again.

He dragged her around the front of the pickup and threw her onto the ground, face first. Her cheek and chin slid through dirt and gravel, leaving considerable skin behind. He put his boot on her neck.

"Now, Theresa." She heard the click of a hammer being cocked. "Remember I told you I'd give you a choice." He let up on the pressure on her neck.

"Look at me!"

She blinked dust out of her eyes and tried to look up, but an unbelievable sight greeted her blurred vision.

Archer! He was stretched out on the ground, his bare torso streaked with dirt. His left hand was stretched out in front of him as if he were reaching for something.

She thought she saw a slight movement, and her heart soared. She blinked and looked again. But he lay deathly still.

What was wrong with his hand? It was black in the pale light of the moon. So was the side of his head. Black streaks marred his cheeks and chin, and dripped down his neck to mix with the dirt.

Blood! It was blood.

"Archer!" she croaked.

"I said look at me!"

Archer's eyes opened—she saw them glittering in the faint moonlight. And she thought he nodded. It was hard to tell with the tears overflowing her own eyes.

She turned her gaze to the monster standing over her. He had his eye on her, but his gun was pointed at Archer.

"So you see that your detective is alive—crippled but alive."

"You sick monster. What did you do to his hand?" She gulped in a sobbing breath. "What do you want from us?"

"What do I want? Oh, so many things, Theresa. You'll find out soon enough." Earl's pulse was hammering so fast it filled his ears like one loud drone. His hands were clammy, and sweat dripped down his neck, tickling his skin as it trickled along his backbone.

He'd never been so excited. The flames inside him made him feel as if he was glowing with heat.

He glanced in Archer's direction. The arrogant former detective was defeated at last. He lay on the ground, his bloody hand stretched helplessly in the direction his gun had flown. He'd groaned when Earl had dumped Theresa on the ground. But he hadn't made a sound since.

This was it. This was the triumph. Now his mom would be proud of him. Now he'd be all over the news.

You'll see me soon, Mom.

He turned back to Theresa, whose wide eyes were flickering back and forth from him to Archer.

"Here's your choice, Theresa. Does your lover get to watch you and me? Or do I kill him now?"

Chapter Thirteen

Archer's head was still groggy, his hand throbbed with every beat of his pulse, and he was having trouble focusing. But he heard the Lock Rapist's words, and they sent hot anger washing over him.

He blinked to clear the blood from his eyes, and studied Resa as well as he could in the dim moonlight.

Her little pink pajamas were ripped and filthy where the bastard had dragged her. Her face was streaked with dirt and tears, as well as blood from several long scrapes. A large dark circle marred her chin. Anger swelled again. The miserable punk had hit her.

He wanted to vault up and knock him to the ground, then pummel him until his face was a bloody mess. But Archer knew he couldn't do that.

He had only one chance, and if he were going to be able to use that chance, he had to stay perfectly still until the Lock Rapist was certain he was no threat.

He knew he was losing blood—too much blood.

And his hand—nauseating horror tasted like bile in his throat. But he swallowed it. He couldn't worry about himself now. He had to save Resa, if it was the last thing he ever did. And it very well could be. Strength was draining out of him as fast as his blood.

He watched helplessly as Resa's attacker grabbed her hair and forced her head back. He leaned down and stuck his face into hers. "I asked you a question."

Resa's eyes filled with tears. "I can't—"

He jerked her head and she cried out.

Archer's whole body tensed, but he couldn't move. Not yet.

"You have to. Which will it be? Do you want to watch Archer die, or would you rather he watched you?"

Archer stared at Resa, willing her to say the right thing. *Me,* he thought at her. *Tell him to kill me first.*

The monster wouldn't do it, but maybe the triumph of hearing her say it would cause him to let down his guard for a few seconds.

Tears streamed down Resa's face, mixing with the dust and dirt. Her wide green eyes met his, and what he saw in them made him want to cry. She believed in him. She believed he could save her.

God help him, he wished *he* believed it.

She closed her eyes and tears spilled over onto her cheeks. "Shoot him," she said, her voice small and broken. "Don't make him suffer."

Archer held his breath. The man turned to look at him, his eyes glittering. Archer met his gaze without lifting his head off the ground. "You pig," he growled, his voice weak.

The man laughed, a weird, high-pitched sound. "Get up, Detective. Get up and fight like a man, why don't you?" He gestured with the gun's barrel.

Archer pulled his useless left hand under him and tried to push his torso off the ground. He groaned and flopped back down.

Resa's eyes turned dark with fear as the Lock Rapist faced her. "There you go. See how well your boyfriend protects you?"

Archer lay there, practicing in his head exactly how he was going to handle the next few moments. He couldn't move too soon, or the attacker would figure out what he was doing. A second too late and Resa would suffer.

The most important thing was that the Lock Rapist not suspect that he'd found his gun. Or that he had it in his right hand, which was positioned between his ribs and the ground.

Moving as little as possible, he adjusted his right hand so that it hurt less. His SIG was ready to fire.

He had no confidence that he'd be able to handle the weapon, much less get off a clean shot. But it was Resa's only chance. His other hand had been ripped to shreds by the Lock Rapist's bullet.

"Get up!" the Lock Rapist yelled at Resa. "Get up on your knees. There ain't no way I'm going to shoot your boyfriend before he gets to see this."

The scrawny punk ripped off his hooded jacket

and began to unbutton his coverall with his left hand. He still held the gun on Archer, but his attention was on the buttons.

"I told you to get up!" he yelled at Resa while he fumbled at the buttons.

Archer took a deep, silent breath and rocked backward. He lifted his hand, grimacing as the shortened tendons strained, and carefully squeezed the trigger. *Don't let the shot go wild.*

He heard a hollow report as if a gun had been fired in another room. Time slowed to a crawl. The Lock Rapist turned his head toward Archer and lifted his weapon. But his hand drooped, his head jerked backward and blood sprayed.

Resa screamed as he crumpled to the ground next to her.

Archer pushed himself to his knees, never taking his eyes off the fallen man. His hand twitched and ached, but with a strength he didn't know he had, he held the gun steady. The monster appeared to be dead, but he couldn't take the risk.

Resa's screams still echoed in his head. But she was crawling toward him, repeating his name over and over.

The screams, he realized, were sirens.

About the time Resa reached him, his knees gave out and he fell against her. She wrapped her arms around his head and shoulders.

The last thing he heard was her voice.

A BLINDING BLUE light flashed in his eyes. He turned his head and tried to raise a hand to block it. But the hand wouldn't move. He tried to lift his other hand but it wouldn't move either.

What the hell?

"Mr. Archer, you need to lie still."

Everything hurt. His head, his hands, his chest. Behind his eyelids, the lights kept flashing. He squinted.

Police cars. Their blue lights were flashing all around him, ramping up the pounding in his head.

Thank God the police were finally here, he thought. But he couldn't remember why.

Odd visions played across his vision in rhythm with the blue lights. A dark shadow darting bizarrely among the cast-iron targets. Clouds obscuring the moon. A lovely, dirty face, streaked with tears. A monster dragging her, hurting her.

Resa! Where was she? He'd failed her again and again. Dear God, don't let him have failed this time.

"Resa!" he cried, trying to sit up.

A firm hand on his chest kept him prone. "Don't try to move."

"Get the hell out of my way," he demanded. "Where is she?" He raised his head and pain stabbed his temples. Then he saw why he couldn't move. He was strapped to the gurney.

He cursed and strained against them. "Get these things off me! I have to get to her!"

The man in white who'd spoken to him loomed over him. "I'm sorry, Mr. Archer, but you've got to calm down. You're going to hurt yourself."

"I'm going to hurt you if you don't let me up!"

Archer saw the man hold up a syringe. "Don't! Get the hell away from me!" He felt a sting in his immobilized arm. "You prick! I've got to find her! She needs me!"

Resa heard Archer's desperate hoarse voice. It ripped right through her. She pushed away the gloved hand that was rubbing an antiseptic wipe across her forehead.

She'd tried several times already to make them let her go to him, but the med techs and the police seemed to be in a conspiracy to keep them apart. He was strapped to a gurney at the door of one ambulance and she was sitting in the open back of another.

"Leave me alone." She batted at the med tech's hand. "There's nothing wrong with me. I want to go with Archer."

The tech glanced toward the other ambulance. "I don't think that's a good idea. We need to check you out before we can release you."

Resa felt frustrated tears spring to her eyes. "I'm fine. But he's not. He's been shot. He needs me." She slapped at the woman's hands.

"I think maybe you need a sedative."

"Don't you dare!"

Several yards away, Clint walked behind a gurney with a covered figure strapped to it. Resa's entire body shuddered at the sight of the black-shrouded corpse.

The monster, the Lock Rapist, was dead. She covered her mouth to stop the sobs of relief.

Gulping in a lungful of air, she cried, "Clint! Detective Banes."

Clint glanced her way. He spoke to the young man in the CSU jacket who was pushing the gurney, then sidestepped it and walked over to the ambulance.

"Resa, how're you doing?" He looked at the med tech. "Has she been processed?"

The tech nodded.

"Clint, what about Archer? Is he all right?"

Clint glanced behind him and Resa saw that two techs were lifting Archer's gurney into the back of the ambulance.

"Where are they taking him? I need to go with him." She turned her head away when the tech tried to apply a bandage to a cut on her forehead.

"Resa, has anyone questioned you yet? I need to know a few things. First and most importantly, did Slattery hurt you?"

Resa stared at Clint. "Slattery? Is that his name? The Lock Rapist?"

Clint nodded grimly.

"Is he dead?"

"Archer shot him in the head."

Resa's heart twisted painfully as the memory hit her. Archer shifting position to reveal the glint of a gun barrel in his hand—his *right* hand. His other hand blood-soaked, useless, unmoving. The hopeless yet determined set to his jaw as he pulled the trigger.

Her breath caught in a sob. "Oh, Clint—his hand. He shot him in the hand."

Clint grimaced. "I know. But the doctors are going to take care of him." He reached out and squeezed her shoulder gently. "Resa, what did Slattery do?"

She watched the ambulance carrying Archer until it disappeared around the front of the house. Then she squeezed her eyes shut as hot tears burned behind them.

"He was a monster. He made me choose." Her throat closed up and her chest ached. "He made me choose," she choked out. "I didn't want to."

"Detective, I think she needs a sedative. She's obviously traumatized."

"Clint, no." Resa grasped his arm. "Please. Don't let them drug me. I need to be with Archer. I need to let him know—"

"Listen to me. The best thing you can do for Geoff right now is to let them give you something to calm you down. We're going to need your statement. Okay?"

"Is he going to be all right?"

Clint reached out and wiped a speck of dirt from her cheek. "I promise you, the doctors are taking very good care of him."

Resa felt the prick of a needle in her arm, but she ignored it. "Please, Clint. Take me to him. I have to explain why I told the Lock Rapist to shoot him. I have to tell him—"

Clint gave her a funny look before turning to the tech. "Drive her to the hospital. Put her with Archer as soon as you can."

To Resa's ears, his voice had started slowing down, like a tape recorder running out of battery. Her head was beginning to swim and her eyes kept wanting to close. She made a huge effort to lift her gaze to Clint's.

"Thank you," she mumbled as the med tech's arm wrapped around her shoulders.

BY THE TIME they rolled Archer into his room, Resa had been there for hours. She'd lain on the couch and napped for a while. She'd showered and changed into scrubs, and she'd given her statement to Detective Childers. She'd told him everything she remembered, and in turn he'd given her the information they had on Earl Slattery, the Lock Rapist.

Resa paced back and forth outside Archer's door until the nurse's aides who'd brought him up from recovery told her she could go back into the room.

He was propped up with pillows and his heavily bandaged left hand was resting on a foam bolster. An IV was attached to his right hand, and a bandage covered the side of his head. His face was shadowed with stubble, which emphasized his paleness.

Resa stared at him. She wanted to touch him, to feel his blood pulsing through his body to assure herself that he was really alive. She'd been so scared. If the Lock Rapist had listened to her—her breath caught in a sob.

"Hey—" His voice was thready, weak. "Resa?"

Resa's breath hitched again. She moved closer to the bed. "Archer? Do you need something?"

His eyes opened to a narrow slit. "You okay?" he whispered.

"Me?" She stared at him. "I'm fine."

He closed his eyes and leaned back against the pillows. "I'm sorry, Resa. I couldn't stop him." He shook his head slightly. "No hero," he whispered.

"But you did. You did stop him." It hurt her to see him so weak and helpless. She knew he was drowsy from the anesthetic as well as the morphine drip, but it was hard, seeing how human he was. How fragile and easily broken his body was. She'd have sworn he was made of steel rather than flesh and bone.

"Can I get you something? Some water?"

He shook his head. "Bastard didn't—hurt you?"

She gently laid her hand over his, the one with the IV. "No," she answered the question he'd implied rather than the one he'd asked. She tried to quash the awful memories of how Slattery had made her crawl. How he'd dragged her by her hair across the yard. How he'd demanded that she kneel in front of him while he unbuttoned his coverall.

"No. He didn't—all he did was pull my hair and push me."

His eyes closed. "Good. Go home."

Resa recoiled as if he'd hit her. "Archer, I'm going to stay here with you."

He forced his eyes open. They were black and intimidating, even if his focus did waver a bit. "I don't need you."

The surprisingly strong words sliced cleanly, right through her heart. "Right. I don't care if you do or not. I'm not leaving."

His dark gaze pinned her. "You got what you wanted. I killed him for you. Now you're free. Go—back to your apartment. Call your sister. It's over." He collapsed back against the pillows, worn out by his outburst.

Resa felt the cool trails of tears on her cheeks. She nodded, swallowing the words that crowded up into her throat.

If she thought it would make any difference, she'd beg him to keep her with him. But she didn't have the strength to hear him say no again.

"I'll go. But I've got something to say first. Don't try to lay your guilt trip at my feet. You could have refused to help me." Her voice gave out. She took a deep breath, sucking in courage.

Archer hadn't moved, hadn't acknowledged that he'd heard anything she'd said, but she knew he had.

"But you were glad to have me, weren't you? I guess I forgot for a while that I was the bait that you dangled in front of the Lock Rapist."

The anger that had fueled her outburst was rapidly fading. And she knew that in a few seconds she'd start to cry.

"You got your vengeance. Now you're going back to bury yourself in your basement again, aren't you? At least this time you've got twice as much reason to feel sorry for yourself. Well, I'm sorry for you if all you can do is wallow in the past." She clenched her trembling hands into fists.

"You're right about one thing, Archer. I'm free. I

just have one last thing to say to you. When I told… him to shoot you, it wasn't because I was afraid of—of dying."

His face hadn't changed expressions, nor had he opened his eyes. Did he even hear her or had he gone to sleep? It didn't matter. What she had to say was about *her* more than him, anyway.

"I knew he was going to kill us both. But I didn't want you to have to watch. You'd been through too much."

She wiped away the tears that were streaming down her face. "Goodbye, Archer. I hope someday you can find something to live for." She sniffled as she stood.

"And for what it's worth, you are a hero." She watched his face for a few seconds, but he never even twitched. So she touched his right hand, just above the IV, and then turned and left.

"You're a world-class jerk, you know that?"

Archer glared at his friend. "Yeah, well, I've been called worse, even by you."

"I don't get you at all. What the hell did you say to her?"

Archer grimaced as he pulled on his shirt. The bandage on his hand barely fit through the sleeve. He stared helplessly at the buttons.

Clint stepped up to him and took hold of his shirt lapels.

"Get away from me."

"Somebody's got to dress you." Clint made quick work of the buttons. "There. Now, I asked you a question. She looked crushed when she left here the other day."

Archer stepped backward, avoiding his friend's eyes. "I told her the truth. I don't need her."

"I take it back. You're worse than a jerk. You're a—" Clint shook his head.

Archer sat down on the bed. His head was throbbing. "I'm a miserable, selfish jerk. Okay? Now get out of here."

"How could you do that to her? She's been through so much."

A queasy, hollow place inside Archer hurt like hell. Worse than his hand. It felt as if Clint had reached inside him and crushed his heart in his fist.

He knew, despite the brave front she'd presented to him, that Resa had been through hell. He'd seen Slattery toss her to the ground and put his boot on her neck. He'd seen him grab her by the hair and get in her face. And he'd watched as he'd forced her to her knees.

"Yeah, she has. And everything that happened to her was because of me. If I hadn't been so arrogant, insisting I could keep her safe, she wouldn't have had to suffer that monster's torture."

"Slattery was a madman. He'd have gotten to her no matter where she was."

"I killed him." Archer shuddered. He'd never killed anyone before. It was one more thing he'd have to live with the rest of his life.

Clint nodded. "You had no choice. It's just too bad he isn't alive to stand trial. We found the original lock of hair in his wallet, along with a lock from his last victim. The district attorney tells me we can connect him to all six attacks, based on that hair. Get this. The lab guys think it was his mother's. They're getting DNA samples to compare."

"What was he doing?"

"We've tracked down police records. His mother was murdered when he was five years old. The shrink says he probably witnessed it. She thinks the killer may have cut a lock of his mother's hair."

"No kidding? That's why he took his victims' hair?"

"Yeah. It doesn't make sense to me, but the shrink says serial offenders can get things like that twisted in their heads. They found videotapes of every mention of the Lock Rapist on TV and every newspaper clipping that mentioned him in a box in the back of his closet. Apparently he had some kind of fixation on seeing or hearing about himself. I guess we'll never know what that was about."

"Well, there's no doubt he was nuts. What about his family?"

Clint shook his head. "Wife and three kids. She had no clue. He left her a note. Told her to buy a big house with his insurance money. Give his kids each a room of their own. He knew he wasn't going to make it."

Archer grimaced. As sick and evil as Slattery had been, he was a human being, with a wife and kids who loved him. Archer would like to think he'd killed a monster, but he knew he would never forget the man's family. Just as he'd never forget Slattery's victims and their families.

He glanced at Clint. "So have you talked to Resa?"

Clint crossed the room to the door. "Last Wednesday. She's gone to Louisville to see her sister."

The hollow empty place inside him ached. He rubbed his chest but it didn't help. "That's good. She loves her sister more than anything."

"She *loves* you."

Archer's head jerked. He felt as if Clint had slugged him. "You're nuts."

"No. You are. You're not going to tell me you don't know."

He shook his head. "You weren't here. You didn't hear what she said to me. I promised her I wouldn't let him hurt her and I didn't keep that promise. She hates me."

"It's too bad that bullet didn't penetrate that hard head of yours. Maybe some sense would have leaked in. There's a hell of a difference between hate and hurt."

"I can't take care of her. I can't protect her. Look at me." He held up his hands.

"Would you get over yourself? Number one, you did protect her. You shot the Lock Rapist—a damn good shot, too, considering it was your right hand. Two, I was there when the surgeon said you'd make a full recovery." He shrugged. "And three, I don't think she wants you just because you can protect her. Why don't you think about *that* for a while? Maybe you'll discover there's more to love than providing protection."

Archer frowned. He wasn't quite sure what his friend was getting at. But he didn't like being told he was wrong—about anything.

"What the heck do you know about love?" he groused.

His friend winced and Archer felt a twinge of guilt. "Look, Clint. Hell—I can be a jerk. I didn't mean to bring that up."

Clint waved a hand. "Forget it." He glanced at his watch.

Archer looked down at himself. His shirt was buttoned, but he still had to get his jeans fastened. And it wasn't going to be easy.

He took a deep breath. "Get the hell out of here, Clint. I need to dress. I'm going home."

Clint's brows lowered. "You mean you're going to rehab? It's only been three days since your surgery."

Archer held up his bandaged hand. "I'll get all the rehab I need at home. You heard the doctor. The bullet went through here, the fleshy part of my palm. It didn't even graze the bone." He smiled dryly. "He said I was lucky it was just a .22 and not something larger. This should heal in no time and be good as new. At least I'll have one hand."

Clint shrugged. "Same old Geoff. Good thing you don't need anybody, 'cause you sure aren't going to listen to them." He sent Archer a look tinged with amusement.

"I'm out of here. Need anything else before I go? Want me to comb your hair? Help you zip up your—"

"No!" Archer couldn't help but smile a little. "You made your point."

"See you later. Think about what I said."

Chapter Fourteen

Resa reached the landing between the first and second floors of her apartment building. She turned to head up the next set of stairs and saw Archer sitting on the top step, his forearms propped on his knees and his head down.

She stopped short, her scalp tingling with apprehension. What was he doing here? She continued slowly up the stairs, pulling her carry-on bag behind her.

She tried not to think about what he wanted. Maybe it was something about the case. Maybe—

He raised his head and she caught an expression she'd never seen before. It was open and oddly vulnerable, as if he were worried about something. The small square bandage on his temple drew her eye.

An uneasy thought sent her heart jumping into her throat. Was it his hand? She looked at the bandage that left only his fingers exposed.

He stood as she reached the top step. He held out his right hand to take her bag.

"Don't bother. I've got it," she said. She ducked around him and pushed the key into the lock and turned it. Inside the door she turned.

He hadn't moved.

She frowned at him. She didn't like this new Archer. He was too quiet, too compliant. She tilted her head. What was his angle?

"Well, aren't you going to come in?" she asked irritably.

"May I?"

She shoved her bag into a corner. "Come on, Archer. Stop the act. I'll bet you never in your life waited to be invited into a place you really wanted to go."

He sent her a pensive look as he crossed the threshold. "I wouldn't say that. There are some places you just don't go without an invitation."

Her cheeks burned at the double meaning of his remark. What was the matter with her? She was positive he hadn't meant anything by it.

He walked around her living room, touching the edge of a painting, stopping to look at a photograph of her and her sister.

He picked it up. "You've been in Louisville, with your mom and your sister?"

She'd followed him with her eyes as he explored the room. She still couldn't pinpoint what wasn't right about him. There was something about the way he was acting that felt—not wrong, exactly. In fact, she thought his obvious unease was kind of endearing.

Still, he wasn't acting like the man she'd come to know so well in the past few weeks.

"Yes."

"Is she doing better? And your mom?"

Resa set her purse down on a chair and lifted her hair off her neck. "Celia is a lot better. You should have seen her when I told her he was dead. It was like the light came back on in her eyes."

He nodded without looking at her. "I'm glad. Clint told me you saw the other victims, too."

"I did. I went with him to let them know that the Lock Rapist was dead. I talked to each one of them for a long time. I told them about Celia, and about—"

"Natalie." He turned and faced her. "That was a good thing you did for them."

"You're acting strange. Is everything all right? Your hand?"

He held up his bandaged left hand. "The doctors say it'll be good as new in a few months. That's more than they ever said for this one." He flexed his right hand.

Good as new. She hoped Archer could be as good as new. He deserved to be.

"I'm glad." She winced internally. She knew now that Earl Slattery was dead, there was no more reason for her and Archer to see each other. They'd been brought together by tragedy and circumstance. Now they'd go their separate ways.

But dear God, she was going to miss him. The thought brought a stinging to her eyes.

"What did you say?" He frowned at her.

"What?" She put her palms to her cheeks. "I'm really tired. I didn't get much sleep at Mom's." She made a show of taking off her summer-weight jacket and laying it across the back of the couch.

Archer leaned against her mantel and watched her, his hawklike eyes glittering in the sunlight that filtered through the curtains.

Finally she propped her fists on her hips and stalked over to stand in front of him.

"Why are you here? Is there something you need from me? I know I still have a few things at your house. I'll pick them up tomorrow if that's all right."

"Resa, stop talking." He straightened.

Even with his bandages, he was formidable. He reached out with his right hand and touched the fading bruise that marred her jawline. For the first few days, she'd made a halfhearted effort to cover it with makeup, but she'd finally decided she didn't really care that it showed.

"I didn't take very good care of you, did I?"

His question shocked her. "Didn't— How can you say that? Archer, you saved my life."

"I never should have brought you to my house. My pride and my cockiness put you in more danger. He targeted you because you were with me." His voice was gruff, his face dark with anger.

But Resa wasn't intimidated. She knew the anger was aimed at himself, not at her. All she wanted to do was throw her arms around him and kiss him. But she couldn't. If he didn't feel the same way, she wasn't sure how she'd cope. It was much better to just keep her mouth shut and let him walk away. At least her pride would be intact.

For all the good that would do her.

"You didn't force me to go to your firing range. I did that all on my own. So it was my fault, not yours. You could say *I* put *you* in danger."

His eyes turned black as deep space. "That's ridiculous. I was supposed to protect you. I had no right to promise you I'd keep you safe."

"Did you come over here to tell me that you failed to meet your own high standards for hero?" He hadn't cornered the market on anger. She'd been highly irritated at him a number of times, but none of them compared to this.

"You're just making excuses," she snapped. "And that's fine. I told you before, go on back to your basement and wallow in your wounded pride and your grief and your anger. But I've got to move on. I have to look forward, not back."

Archer took a step closer to her but she held up her hand. "I'm sorry you feel like you lost everything. If I were in your place I'd probably feel that way, too."

She took a step forward and raised her chin, putting her face no more than a foot from his. "But do you seriously believe you're not a hero? If that's true, you'd better look around. You're one of a kind, Geoffrey Archer."

All the anger drained out of her, leaving her feeling

empty and alone. She backed away, needing distance. His dark eyes were burning her skin.

She turned away and picked up her jacket, making a show of folding it and picking a piece of lint off it. "You should go home. I'm going to go to bed early. I've got a lot of catching up to do to have all my clients' dresses finished before the country music awards ceremony in August."

Behind her, Archer didn't move. She closed her eyes briefly, then headed toward her bedroom with her jacket and carry-on bag.

"Resa?"

She stopped at the door without turning around. Something in his voice sent a spear of loneliness through her. Suddenly, even if she'd wanted to, turning around wasn't an option. She couldn't face him with her eyes spilling over with tears. She set her jaw, ignoring the drops tickling her cheeks as they ran down. She was determined not to reach up and wipe them away while he was looking at her.

She'd feel better in the morning. She was just tired, that was all. As soon as he left, she'd climb into bed and have a good cry and a good nap and by tomorrow everything would be fine.

Or at least better.

"Come home."

She'd thought he'd said *come home.* She'd misunderstood him. Hadn't she?

She ducked her head and swiped at the tears. Then she turned around.

"Pardon me?" Her voice sounded choked, as if her heart were beating faster than a drumroll. It was.

His mouth curled slightly, but his eyes held wariness. "I'd like for you to come home."

"Home?" She took a deep breath, but it caught in her throat. "Archer, don't play with me. I'm too tired. Too—"

"I would never play with your heart," he said solemnly.

Resa's face turned white.

Archer held his breath. He'd found out from her mother when she'd be back, and he hadn't slept a wink last night. He'd faced Resa a hundred times, asked her the same thing a hundred different ways, but that was practice. This was for real.

And he was scared spitless. He hadn't realized how thoroughly she'd gotten under his skin. How completely she'd taken over his life, how she'd become as necessary to him as the air he breathed.

He hadn't realized how much he loved her.

"What?" Resa's face grew paler, if that were possible. Her deep-green eyes widened.

Had he said that aloud? His heart felt as though it had dropped to his feet, and his chest tightened until he was afraid he wouldn't be able to speak.

"I guess—" He swallowed and started over. "I guess I said I didn't realize how much I love you."

She didn't move.

His throat quivered. Damn. Facing bad guys was a picnic compared to this. He'd been closed off for so long, he'd forgotten how to be tender, how to woo a woman. "I'm not handling this very well."

She didn't say anything.

Not handling it well? Hell, he sucked at it. He rubbed the back of his neck.

"No—" she croaked in a small voice. "No, you're doing fine."

He took a step toward her. "It's been a long time."

She nodded, her gaze never leaving his. "I know."

"So what do you say?" His mouth was so dry he could hardly speak.

"What are you asking?" She took a step toward him.

He shrugged and spread his hands. "So would you want to get married?"

To his surprise, she laughed and stepped into the circle of his arms. "Archer, you make a wonderful hero but you suck at romance."

He kissed her cheek, tasting the salty flavor of her tears. "I'll trust you to teach me."

* * * * *

A riveting new thriller
by acclaimed author

LAURA CALDWELL

When Liza sets up the newly divorced Kate
with Michael Waller, neither woman
expects Kate to fall for him so soon. The
relationship is a whirlwind that enthralls
Kate…and frightens Liza. Because Liza
knows she may have introduced Kate to
more than her dream man; she may have
unwittingly introduced her to a dangerous
world of secrets. Secrets that steer the
women's friendship on an international
collision course, rife with betrayals that
could cause the end of all of them.

THE GOOD LIAR

"A taut international thriller certain to
keep readers breathless and awake until
the wee hours of the morning."
—James Rollins, *New York Times*
bestselling author of *Map of Bones*

*Available the first week of January 2008
wherever paperbacks are sold!*

www.MIRABooks.com

MIRA®

MLC2501

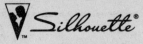

Romantic
SUSPENSE

Sparked by Danger,
Fueled by Passion.

When Tech Sergeant Jacob "Mako" Stone opens
his door to a mysterious woman without a past,
he knows his time off is over. As threats to Dee's
life bring her and Jacob together, she must set
aside her pride and accept the help of the military
hero with too many secrets of his own.

Out of Uniform
by Catherine Mann

Available February wherever you buy books.

REQUEST YOUR FREE BOOKS!

2 FREE NOVELS PLUS 2 FREE GIFTS!

◆ HARLEQUIN®
INTRIGUE®

Breathtaking Romantic Suspense

YES! Please send me 2 FREE Harlequin Intrigue® novels and my 2 FREE gifts. After receiving them, if I don't wish to receive any more books, I can return the shipping statement marked "cancel." If I don't cancel, I will receive 6 brand-new novels every month and be billed just $4.24 per book in the U.S., or $4.99 per book in Canada, plus 25¢ shipping and handling per book and applicable taxes, if any*. That's a savings of close to 15% off the cover price! I understand that accepting the 2 free books and gifts places me under no obligation to buy anything. I can always return a shipment and cancel at any time. Even if I never buy another book from Harlequin, the two free books and gifts are mine to keep forever.

182 HDN EEZ7   382 HDN EEZK

Name _____ (PLEASE PRINT) _____

Address _____ Apt. # _____

City _____ State/Prov. _____ Zip/Postal Code _____

Signature (if under 18, a parent or guardian must sign)

Mail to the **Harlequin Reader Service®**:
IN U.S.A.: P.O. Box 1867, Buffalo, NY 14240-1867
IN CANADA: P.O. Box 609, Fort Erie, Ontario L2A 5X3

Not valid to current Harlequin Intrigue subscribers.

Want to try two free books from another line?
Call 1-800-873-8635 or visit www.morefreebooks.com.

* Terms and prices subject to change without notice. NY residents add applicable sales tax. Canadian residents will be charged applicable provincial taxes and GST. This offer is limited to one order per household. All orders subject to approval. Credit or debit balances in a customer's account(s) may be offset by any other outstanding balance owed by or to the customer. Please allow 4 to 6 weeks for delivery.

Your Privacy: Harlequin is committed to protecting your privacy. Our Privacy Policy is available online at www.eHarlequin.com or upon request from the Reader Service. From time to time we make our lists of customers available to reputable firms who may have a product or service of interest to you. If you would prefer we not share your name and address, please check here. ☐

the DEVIL'S footprints

Don't miss
the latest thriller from

AMANDA STEVENS

On sale March 2008!

AMANDA STEVENS

the DEVIL'S footprints

MARKED BY EVIL...

SAVE $1.00 off the purchase price of **THE DEVIL'S FOOTPRINTS** by Amanda Stevens.

Offer valid from March 1, 2008 to May 31, 2008. Redeemable at participating retail outlets. Limit one coupon per purchase.

52608155

65373 00076 2   (8100) 0 11460

MAS2530CPN

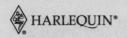

HARLEQUIN®

INTRIGUE®

COMING NEXT MONTH

#1041 POINT BLANK PROTECTOR by Joanna Wayne
Four Brothers of Colts Run Cross
When Kali Cooper inherits the Silver Spurs Ranch, she isn't prepared to find a murdered woman there, or the wealthy rancher next door. But Zach Collingsworth can be counted on when all the chips are down—and it looks like it's Kali's time to cash in.

#1042 GUARDIAN ANGEL by Debra Webb
Colby Agency
No one knows who the Guardian Angel is or where he comes from. But to rescue six missing children, investigator Ann Martin will have to break her own rules and trust a vigilante who operates on the other side of the law.

#1043 UNDER HIS SKIN by Rita Herron
Nighthawk Island
Nurse Grace Gardener brings Parker Kilpatrick back from the brink of death, only to seek his protection. On a collision course with two killers who want their secrets kept, Grace recruits the one detective with the brass to stop them.

#1044 NEWBORN CONSPIRACY by Delores Fossen
Five-Alarm Babies
Mia Crandall and Logan McGrath are about to have a baby. Except they have never met. Now they must work together to save their child, but can they survive the frightening conspiracy behind their unplanned union?

#1045 SET UP WITH THE AGENT by Lori L. Harris
With her cover blown, China Benedict is targeted for death. But she survives. Now FBI counterterrorism expert Killian James will put his life on the line to keep China out of harm's way in order to recover a stolen biological weapon.

#1046 FORBIDDEN TOUCH by Paula Graves
Away from the prying eyes of the world, Iris Browning and Maddox Heller are both looking to bury their secrets. Instead they find each other. Yet the closer they get, the more dangerous their attraction becomes—until it isn't something either can easily walk away from.

www.eHarlequin.com

HICNM0108